Tara Moss is a bestselling author, human rights activist, documentary host, and model. Her novels have been published in nineteen countries and thirteen languages, and her memoir *The Fictional Woman* was a #1 national bestseller. She is a UNICEF Goodwill Ambassador and has received the Edna Ryan Award for her significant contributions to feminist debate and for speaking out for women and children, and in 2017 she was recognised as one of the Global Top 50 Diversity Figures in Public Life. She is a PhD Candidate at the University of Sydney, and has earned her private investigator credentials (Cert III) from the Australian Security Academy. *The Cobra Queen* is her thirteenth book and fourth Pandora English novel.

Also by Tara Moss

FICTION
The Pandora English series
The Blood Countess
The Spider Goddess
The Skeleton Key
The Cobra Queen

The Makedde Vanderwall series
Fetish
Split
Covet
Hit
Siren
Assassin

The Billie Walker series
Dead Man Switch (The War Widow)

NON-FICTION
The Fictional Woman
Speaking Out

TARA MOSS

THE SKELETON KEY

echo

Echo Publishing
An imprint of Bonnier Books UK
80-81 Wimpole Street
London W1G 9RE
www.echopublishing.com.au
www.bonnierbooks.co.uk

First published by Pan Macmillan Australia in 2012.
This edition first published by Echo Publishing in 2020.

Cover design by Lisa Brewster
Typesetting and reformatting by Shaun Jury

Typeset in Baskerville

Printed in Australia at Griffin Press.
Only wood grown from sustainable regrowth forests is used in the
manufacture of paper found in this book.

NATIONAL LIBRARY OF AUSTRALIA

A catalogue record for this book is available from the
National Library of Australia
ISBN: 9781760685881 (paperback)
ISBN: 9781760686550 (ebook)

 echopublishingau

 echo_publishing

 echo_publishing

For Berndt

CHAPTER ONE

*I*t was near the end of the working day as I cast an uneasy glance at my watch and then at the empty office behind me. Manhattan was preparing for another sunset. Another sunset meant another stretch of night and with the night came the darkness, and the creatures of the night.

My boss would be along anytime.

At the thought, I shivered. I was pretty sure she'd been infected with a bad dose of undead.

I sat in my little cubicle at *Pandora* magazine in SoHo, where I worked as a lowly assistant to the editor. The office was chic and sparsely furnished, with several large cubicles spread out across the open-plan space, and one walled office built into the corner. That office belonged to my boss, Skye DeVille. (The one who had stopped showing up during daylight hours. Suspicious.) I dutifully finished checking the constant influx of emails for my absent boss and at five o'clock I shut my computer down. It hummed for a moment, something whirring inside, then fell silent. Leaning back in my chair, I looked both ways, and on seeing that I was unobserved, I reached into the leather satchel at my feet and pulled out the small object that was secreted there, in an inside pocket.

I placed the object on my desk in front of the keyboard. It was perhaps three or four inches long, carved out of some kind of metal, and it had the dappled patina of over a century of wear. My great-aunt had given it to me.

The skeleton key.

Come on. Try it again, I told myself.

I stared at the key and licked my lips.

You can do it.

Leaning my elbows on the edge of the desk, shielded by the walls of the cubicle, I brought my fingertips to my temples and concentrated. I closed my eyes and tried to feel the key with my mind, tried to reach out with my senses. The seconds passed slowly and in time the sounds of the office around me faded to a low murmur. The room seemed to disappear and when my mind was clear of every distraction I opened my eyes again, squinting, and I focused on the key. *Only the skeleton key. Nothing else. Everything is the skeleton key. The skeleton key is everything . . . and I can control it . . .*

Gradually, after perhaps one agonising minute, the skeleton key began to vibrate, began to shift diagonally . . .

'What are you up to tonight? Anything fun?'

A voice broke my concentration and I looked up, startled. The skeleton key hit the edge of my desk and fell into my lap. My friend Morticia had abandoned her post as office receptionist to visit me. She's my friend, maybe my only truly 'normal' friend in New York.

(Despite her name, which she changed from Bea to spite her conservative parents.) I pushed my chair back from my cubicle and tucked a long lock of light brown hair behind my ear. My face felt hot.

'What's that?'

'Just a key,' I told her, and quickly slipped it back in the satchel.

'So, what are you up to? You look like you're up to something.'

'Do I?'

'You've been grinning all day.'

Morticia perched herself on the edge of my desk, folding one leg over the other. She had shaggy red hair the colour of food dye, a lopsided smile, big eyes and long gangly legs. Imagine Popeye's girlfriend Olive Oyl – as a goth. As usual she wore a black dress, striped tights and Doc Martens. It was like a uniform for her, though it certainly didn't help her to blend in with the magazine's other staff. I kind of admired the fact that she didn't care about that.

I found myself grinning at the thought of the night ahead. *What am I up to tonight? Well . . .*

'Actually, I'm going on a date,' I blurted, and then immediately regretted it.

Morticia's eyes widened, her black pencilled eyebrows sitting up like little accents. 'Oh, look at your face! Are you blushing, Pandora?'

Yes, I was blushing. And, yes, my late mother, the archaeologist, and my late father, the academic, had seen fit to name their only child after the woman in Greek mythology who opened a box and let all the evil into the world. (Actually, I think it was an urn, not a box, but never mind.) Morticia and I work at *Pandora*, and although it can sound impressive when I get to introduce myself as 'Pandora English of *Pandora* magazine', the depressing reality is that I fetch a lot of coffee and Chai tea for the editor – she of the stroppy attitude, increasingly nocturnal habits and undead-style OCD (a common issue, apparently) – and I sift through emails and take messages. The fact is, I'm nineteen years old and I've never worked in publishing before so just having my foot in the door of the publishing world is something I'm grateful for regardless of the ... well, the complications with my boss.

I looked anxiously at the darkening skies outside the window and found myself absent-mindedly touching the antique ring on my finger. The jet-black obsidian stone was held in place by delicate gold claws, and in the centre of that stone there always seemed to be some small, blazing pinpoint of light.

'Where is your date taking you?' Morticia pressed. 'Dinner? A movie?'

I thought about the night ahead. 'I think we'll be, um, sightseeing,' I replied vaguely. I couldn't help it. I started grinning again.

The truth was, my date wasn't taking *me* anywhere. Though technically I was the one who was new in town, having only been here three months, my friend Lieutenant Luke hadn't seen the sights of midtown Manhattan before. Not in the flesh, anyway. I planned to show him the view from the top of the Empire State Building and I'd been looking forward to this opportunity all month. It was set to be a spectacular evening. This was the night of the Full Worm Moon, or Full Crow Moon, when the crows cast their calls and the earthworms appear, signalling the end of winter. (Since moving in with my great-aunt Celia I'd been learning things like that.) I had mixed feelings about the change of seasons, as winter's shorter days had meant longer nights. Considering some of the problems I'd been having after dark, you'd think I'd be delighted by the changes spring would bring. And in a way I was. But when the nights became shorter, there would also be fewer hours I could spend with Luke.

'What is it?' Morticia asked.

'Nothing.'

'You're not going to tell me about your date?'

'Maybe if it goes well,' I offered, as a form of deflection.

The last time I'd told her about a date of mine, things had gone badly. Not for any complicated romantic reasons, but because of what you might call supernatural amnesia. Jay Rockwell – known by Morticia only as 'roses guy' – was the only person I'd dated in New York. The last time I'd spoken to him, by phone, I had been terribly embarrassed to discover that he knew nothing of me or our brief time together. What could I do? Explain to him that he'd been erased to protect supernatural secrets? No. And even though I kind of wanted to, I really couldn't tell Morticia about Lieutenant Luke, either. He wasn't a regular guy. It was far too complicated to explain and I wasn't sure it would be a good idea to even try. We had more pressing things to chat about, anyway.

'Do you think she'll ... um, come in soon?' I asked.

I looked at my boss's office again and Morticia shrugged. 'Skye has been coming in later and later, hasn't she? Weird.'

And the days are becoming longer, I thought.

'It's odd, isn't it?' I agreed, and bit my lip.

Skye DeVille had been keeping strange hours and I had every reason to be worried about what that meant. Though Morticia and some of the other staff had noticed Skye's increasingly odd routines, I doubted they would understand the potential significance. But I didn't want to think about all that now. Not when I was about to have a very important night out with Lieutenant Luke. I wanted to be at home when he arrived. The weeks of anticipation had felt like much longer.

'I'm on a bit of a tight schedule tonight,' I said anxiously. 'I can't really work late.'

'Exactly! Just because she's working late all the time now doesn't mean you have to!' Morticia offered, though it didn't quite ring true.

I was Skye's assistant, after all, and I'd been left in no doubt of my position at the office. I was placed well below her and the ice-blonde deputy editor Pepper Smith, who had been taking up the slack recently, with Skye's absences. In the office hierarchy I was somewhere between Morticia and the pesky office rat, for whom poisoned bait was regularly put out. Yup, you could say I was pretty low on the corporate ladder, so if I was gone every time my boss put in an appearance at work … well, that just couldn't be a good thing. Skye could be pretty unpleasant, but I needed this job. I couldn't be totally reliant on the generosity of my great-aunt. That just wouldn't be right.

'I can walk with you to the subway if you're leaving soon,' I said. It was ten past five now. I had to get moving. In fact, if I stayed even ten more minutes I'd probably have to splurge on a cab to save time.

'I'll be here another twenty minutes, I think,' Morticia replied.

I certainly couldn't wait that long if I hoped to be home before sundown.

'Well, I should head off. I told Pepper yesterday that I had to leave at five today.' I stood up and straightened my clothes. 'See you tomorrow, Morticia.' I threw on my coat and picked up my satchel.

'By the way, your makeup looks real pretty lately. What is it, bronzer?' Morticia asked, following me across the office.

I shrugged. 'I haven't been doing anything new. Must be the light in here.'

'Well, you look really great anyway. Kind of glowy.'

My excitement about seeing Luke obviously showed. That was kind of embarrassing.

'Hey, good luck tonight!' Morticia declared as I left her at the reception desk and made for the door. 'I hope it's a killer date.'

I flinched.

I really hoped it wasn't one of those. Again.

'Pandora!' came a voice. It was Pepper. She rushed over, evidently with a mind to stop me leaving. Pepper was slim and wiry, built like a distance athlete, and today she wore skinny leather-look trousers and a long top made out of some sort of jersey, the bottom of it twisted into stylish knots. Her hair was gelled back and fashionably severe, and when she stopped in front of me not one strand of it appeared to move. I didn't know what to make of her, except that she was smart, competitive and highly strung, and we didn't see eye to eye on intellectual copyright. (She'd basically stolen an entire piece I'd done on an infamous beauty cream scam, and published it with barely a credit. *Additional reporting by Pandora English. Ha!*)

I stood my ground and back at reception Morticia's eyes widened a little, like I might be in trouble.

'I mentioned yesterday that I had to leave at five,' I reminded Pepper.

'Oh yeah. That's fine. I just want to tell you I need you to cover a party on Saturday night for our social page,' she said to my surprise. 'You do have time, don't you?'

'A party? Like a product launch?' I'd covered one of those before.

'It's a big annual party. All the important people in New York will be there. I'll be there, of course,' she said, as if it were obvious that she fit that description.

'You'd like me to go with you?'

Pepper laughed. 'Lord no. I need you to take photos. Do you have a camera?'

I frowned. I only had my phone camera.

'Well, I have one you can borrow anyway. I'll give it to you tomorrow along with your media pass.'

'What are you looking for exactly?'

'The usual celebrity happy snaps. It's not rocket science.'

I nodded. 'Okay.' My eyes went to the clock again. 'Well, I'd better go,' I said, but Pepper was already walking back to her desk.

There was no sign of Skye DeVille as I stepped out onto the busy streets of SoHo. I noticed the Evolution shop next door was overflowing with customers. A full-sized skeleton stood out front holding a sale sign in its bony fingers, swaying a little on medical-grade plastic joints. Manhattan rush hour sure took some getting used to, though I have to admit that most hours still seemed like rush hour to me after growing up in sleepy Gretchenville (population 3999 after my unprecedented departure). But on this particular afternoon the footpath outside the *Pandora* office did seem particularly packed. Men and women in trendy clothes and slick suits pushed past me in both directions, each one of them on a determined mission to be somewhere else. Someone in that faceless crowd bumped into me and my leather satchel fell off my shoulder.

I adjusted it and looked up at the sun. It sat low in the sky.

Luke.

Could I get home in time by my usual subway route?

That meant crossing Central Park, and that might take a touch too long. But cabs were expensive, especially considering how far uptown I needed to travel. It was kind of off the map.

I was just considering my options when I noticed a long, black car through a gap in the pedestrians. The car was parked and the back door was open, waiting for a passenger. A toweringly tall man, as pale as parchment, stood next to it. He wore dark sunglasses, an impeccable black suit and black shoes that shone in the early evening light. His pallor and deathlike stillness were unnerving. And familiar.

'Hi, Vlad,' I said.

He didn't speak. I had never heard him speak.

I shook my head and smiled to myself as I slid onto the comfortable upholstery in the back seat of Celia's car. Vlad shut the door for me. My great-aunt knew about my date and she'd sent her chauffeur to get me home on time. This sort of thing happened with some regularity, though I tried to discourage it. Great-Aunt Celia was already providing me with a wonderful room and hospitality, and she insisted on picking up the tab for my groceries. I didn't want her chauffeur to ferry me around, too. It was too much. But this evening was special, so I strapped myself in without protest. 'Thank you,' I told Vlad as he started the car.

In moments we pulled away from the kerb into the flow of traffic with a smoothness I would have thought impossible. Before long we were out of SoHo and on our way uptown along Madison Avenue, where I pressed my face to the car window and gazed out at the passing spectacle of stores and skyscrapers. We slowed occasionally in patches of congested traffic but managed to hit the Upper East Side in good time, passing row upon row of houses that were so tightly knit that the population of a single block was probably higher than the entire population of my hometown.

Eventually we pulled into the green expanse of Central Park, the famous Manhattan oasis where the recent arrival of spring gave everything a fresh dash of colour. On either side of the road, flowers were already budding and the trees looked luscious and full. The sight filled me with cheer. Vlad turned down a single-lane road in the park and as we approached the little tunnel that led to home, the car was enveloped by a thick fog. For a moment I couldn't see beyond the car's windscreen, let alone past the headlights.

Spektor is always surrounded by fog. And it doesn't appear on any map (or GPS). I'd found these facts peculiar at first, but it is amazing what you can get used to when your reality requires it.

Presently we emerged from the wall of fog to find ourselves on the quiet main street of Spektor, where a light mist clung to the old buildings. We passed Harold's Grocer, which was open day and night, and pulled up at Number One Addams Avenue, a large mansion in the heart of the suburb.

Home spooky home.

Vlad opened the door for me and I stepped out, clutching my satchel. 'Thanks so much,' I said.

Vlad was perhaps a full foot taller than me and I found myself staring at him for a moment. His face was pale, placid and expressionless. *He is so still*, I observed. If he breathed, I couldn't tell. In the reflection of his dark sunglasses I could see that the sun was starting to set, its radiance filtered through layers of light mist.

'Well, um, thanks again,' I said awkwardly and scurried towards the big iron gates at the front door.

I had perhaps twenty minutes.

CHAPTER
TWO

*N*umber One Addams Avenue was built in the 1880s in neo-Gothic style. It towered over the other buildings of Spektor, its embellished arches, turrets and spikes stretching up to the sky. In time, the stonework of the great mansion had faded to stained variations of grey, but the imposing nature of the building remained. It stood a proud five storeys high and took up most of a small city block. Designed by the infamous Victorian-era architect and psychical researcher Dr Edmund Barrett, it was said to house twisting passageways and a hidden laboratory where many mysterious experiments had taken place before Dr Barrett's untimely death. It was clear the mansion had seen better days, but though the windows on the middle floors were boarded up, giving it a slightly abandoned air, it would be wrong to assume those floors were uninhabited.

Soon those who slept beyond those covered windows would wake.

Given the opportunity, it was advisable to get home before this occurred. My timing was good.

I slid my house key into the lock, and after a murmured word of encouragement, managed to open the heavy wooden front door. The entry lobby always seemed to have a tomblike chill and I pulled my collar close as I stepped inside. Perhaps it would warm up a bit come summer? There was little doubt this entry area would have once been grand. It boasted a high ceiling, beautiful tilework and a lift encased in an intricate — if broken — cage of ironwork. A circular staircase to one side snaked up to a mezzanine floor, barred by a large door I had not yet managed to open. Above me, the large lobby chandelier was impressive, though it hung askew, draped in layers of cobwebs and dust.

At the sight of it I rolled my eyes.

I'd lost count of the number of times I'd taken out my great-aunt's ladder and straightened that chandelier. How many times had I dusted it and carefully wiped down the heavy, tear-shaped crystals? There had to be a draft somewhere, pushing the dust around. It was disappointing, but never mind.

Schraaack.

I took a step across the lobby and stopped.

Thrrrraaaaaaaack.

There it was again. I'd heard those sounds before, always in the lobby. Was it something beneath the floor? A kind of movement? A trick of acoustics? I couldn't identify the source of the noise and it seemed that every time I stopped to concentrate on it, the house grew quiet again. Like it knew that I was listening. But tonight was special and precious time was passing, I reminded myself.

I made my way towards the old-fashioned lift, my heels clicking on the tiles. The elevator was waiting for me on the lobby floor and as soon as I pushed the call button, the doors opened with a squeak. I didn't hear any weird noises from the lift, and I didn't want to think about them for the moment anyway. Mind firmly on the evening ahead, I took the elevator to the top floor, watching the dusty landings pass as I went. I hadn't attempted to clean those landings; it seemed decidedly unwise considering the others who lived on the middle floors. Plus, it wasn't really *my* job, was it?

On the top floor, I stepped up to the big midnight-blue doors of my great-aunt Celia's penthouse. Knocking first was one of my great-aunt's rules. I rapped my knuckles on the old door, slid my key in and stepped inside.

'Hi, Great-Aunt Celia. I'm home,' I declared cheerily.

The penthouse was warm and comforting as I entered. I hung my coat on the mirrored Edwardian coat stand and slipped off my heeled shoes, sinking a couple of inches.

Celia's penthouse still had the power to take my breath away. It was a remarkable space, with high domed ceilings and sparking chandeliers. Unlike the chandelier downstairs, these ones – and in fact the entire penthouse – never collected dust. The floors of the penthouse were gleaming polished wood and the main room in which I now stood was filled with rows of bookcases holding thick, mysterious tomes, some in languages I didn't even recognise. Each item of furniture was antique – Victorian, Edwardian, art deco. Tables and chairs bore animals and mythical creatures, carved into the wood. Glass-fronted sideboards held artefacts as varied and curious as any museum's. A carved tusk. A Venus flytrap. A two-headed coin. Fertility statues. An art deco nymph. Butterflies and moths in gleaming glass domes. A live black widow spider in a glass cage. (That last item made me shudder.)

Tonight Celia had the curtains open over the tall, arched windows to reveal a crimson and maroon sunset, set against the spectacular Manhattan skyline. The Empire State Building stood out, silhouetted in black. Soon I would be there with Luke, enjoying the view, I hoped.

My great-aunt was seated, as usual, under the halo of her reading light in the lovely nook where she spent much of her time, surrounded by her books. I could see her elbow, and then she peeked her head around the corner.

'Good evening, Pandora. What very good timing you have. The Crow Moon will rise soon,' she said.

She had her feet up on the leather hassock and, next to it, her cat Freyja was curled up. Freyja was pure white, an albino, with beautiful opal-coloured eyes. She lifted her head and purred at me contentedly, then snuggled into her furry paws again. She must have had a big day of adventure to be so tired.

'The moon will be spectacular,' I agreed and nodded enthusiastically. There was just enough time to quickly shower and change. I didn't want to miss a minute of the evening ahead. 'You didn't need to send Vlad,' I told my great-aunt. 'It's too generous of you.'

'But you wouldn't have arrived in time for sunset,' she replied calmly, forever pragmatic.

'Still ...' I began.

My great-aunt's slim ankles were encased in fine stockings – she always wore the kind with the line up the back – and now she uncrossed her ankles and slipped her feet into a pair of elegant, heeled slippers. She leaned forward and placed a feather in her book to mark the faded page. It was a leather-bound tome and one, I imagined, filled with great knowledge. She swung herself around and regarded me.

Despite working at a fashion magazine I don't know a whole lot about the fashion world, but, lucky for me, my great-aunt Celia is an unusually stylish woman. She was once a designer to the stars of Hollywood's Golden Era and she was never seen in anything less than an ensemble worthy of the pages of *Vogue* – 1940s *Vogue*, specifically. Tonight she was wearing an emerald-green silk dress, cut on the bias, a thin black leather belt circling her willowy waist. Partially obscuring her face was a black widow's veil, positioned at an angle over her jet-black locks. Celia did not like to be seen without her veil. Her husband, a photographer, had died many decades before and I supposed she remembered him with some fondness. Still, it seemed an eccentric habit. Beneath the mesh of the veil my great-aunt's cheekbones were high and sculpted. Her lips were painted in a blood-red lipstick and her skin was as smooth as a pearl. Which is odd, as by my calculations she should be nearly ninety. This fact had caused some suspicion from me early on in our friendship, but I'd now pretty much grown used to this odd characteristic of hers. And others.

Celia had encouraged me to apply for the position at *Pandora* after I'd been rejected by other publications. Somehow she'd just known I'd get this job.

She has a spooky way of knowing things.

'Oh, you know I have to keep Vlad busy,' my great-aunt said, dismissing my protest with a wave of her manicured hand. 'Where will you go tonight?' She tilted her head and waited.

I grinned. 'The Empire State Building. We'll walk.'

'Oh, that will be a pleasant stroll,' Celia said. 'Do you think he'll be able to get there okay?'

I knew what she meant.

'I think so. I feel positive about it,' I said. She'd been encouraging me to go with my instincts and my instincts told me that tonight would be a breakthrough.

'Good. Well, that should make for a very interesting evening then. Be sure to wear something warm in case it gets chilly.'

I thought of Celia's vintage fox stole. She'd been wearing it for decades and it did rather suit her, but though she'd offered to let me borrow it I didn't feel all that comfortable wearing a whole animal around my neck. Maybe that was hypocritical of me, considering I wasn't even a vegetarian.

'The fox stole is on the coat stand if you want it,' she said.

I thought I detected the tiniest hint of mischief in her voice. Sometimes I swear Celia knows what I'm thinking.

'That's okay. Thanks anyway. I'd better get ready now,' I told her and started walking to my room.

'Deus wishes to see you tonight,' she said, just as I had my hand on the doorknob.

I stopped and turned. 'Really? Deus?' At the thought, my mouth became dry.

It had been one month since I'd last seen Deus, on the night he'd saved me from falling off the roof. It had been a complicated situation but, suffice it to say, I was pretty uncomfortable about owing him my life. Deus was very close to Celia, that was true, but still, he was *Sanguine*. You know – an undead person. Sanguine means *of blood*. The V word is very politically incorrect, and I don't recommend using it unless you'd like to get necked.

Deus was a very busy creature. And ancient. And pretty important from what I could tell. A meeting with him was no small thing. It almost certainly meant that something serious was up.

'Do you know what he, um, wants to see me about?'

'He says he needs to tell you in person.'

'Oh,' I said.

'You go ahead and have a good time with your soldier tonight. If you're back around midnight he'll see you then,' my great-aunt said.

She said this as a statement. Not a possibility. I'd be back at midnight then.

I went to my room and showered quickly in the ensuite, being careful not to wet my hair, then laid out some of my favourite clothes on my four-poster bed. My great-aunt had a stunning wardrobe and she was always giving me things to wear. I'd arrived from Gretchenville with barely the clothes on my back, and even those had not been very nice, but by now I had borrowed quite a collection of vintage dresses and tops. Incredibly, everything of Great-Aunt Celia's fitted me, even the shoes. She said it was because I was a Lucasta, like her. If surnames were not so unwaveringly patriarchal, I would have been Pandora Lucasta instead of Pandora English, as Lucasta was my mother's maiden name. Lucasta women are always the same size, Celia claimed. Lucasta women also had a few other things in common. They each had different 'gifts', as Celia called them.

My unusual abilities sure hadn't seemed like gifts when I was growing up. My father had admonished me for having an 'overactive imagination', and after I predicted the death of the local butcher and claimed to be in contact with him after he passed, people stopped visiting our family house. I was branded with the 'weird kid' tag and that was even before my parents died in an accident in Egypt when I was eleven. After that I was sent to live with my well-meaning but rather strict aunt Georgia, my dad's sister. She was the local maths teacher in Gretchenville and not very popular. And she was even less tolerant than my father had been of my little 'quirks'.

Aunt Georgia even insisted on calling me Dora to save me the embarrassment of being named after the woman who was the 'cause of all sin'. (Please don't call me Dora. I beg you.) Truthfully, I had no hope of fitting in and my whole world was turned upside down when Great-Aunt Celia, my only other relative, invited me to live with her in Manhattan a few months ago. I'd imagined I'd be looking after a geriatric. How wrong I'd been.

I'd never even met Celia before she'd sent me that letter. Now I wondered how I'd ever lived without her.

For a moment I stood in my bedroom in Celia's penthouse in a towel, my arms folded, considering my options. In only five minutes I had changed outfits three times. My date would not have cared how I was dressed, but I suppose I was nervous. Lieutenant Luke was always formally dressed. (He didn't have much choice about that.) This was also the first time we were technically going *out* together so it felt like too special an occasion to simply wear my favourite jeans and T-shirt. In the end I decided on a simple but perfectly tailored silk dress, a sapphire-blue one my great-aunt had designed in the early 1950s. It buttoned at the chest and had a pussy bow at the neck, and the hem fell to just above my knees. I wore it with a pair of drop earrings and a comfortable pair of ballet flats. The flats were good walking shoes.

I examined my reflection in the mirror on the oak dresser and patted down my naturally light brown hair. Good. It was pretty much under control. I stepped closer to my reflection. Funny, but now that Morticia had mentioned it, I could see that I did have a bit of a tan.

I guess I'd been walking a lot to and from work. Should I bother with lipstick even though I hoped it wouldn't stay on for long? Perhaps not. I frowned. Okay, maybe just a little. I patted on some red lip gloss with a finger and rubbed my lips together. The colour made my amber eyes a little brighter.

Butterflies. There were butterflies in my stomach.

The sun had set, and now the moon's strength could be seen outside the open windows. I thought I felt it, too. There was an electricity in the atmosphere.

Without further pause I cleared the clothes from my bed and straightened the covers out of habit. Then I knelt on the hardwood floor. A sword sat under the bed, wrapped in a thick velvet stretch of cloth. I grabbed it by the grip just below the hand guard and pulled it out. Carefully, I unwrapped the cloth to reveal the gleaming blade. The sword had a gentle curve and it was engraved with the initials of its owner.

L.T.

It was Second Lieutenant Luke Thomas's cavalry sword. Holding it tightly by the grip, I stood up, closed my eyes and took a deep breath. 'Lieutenant Luke,' I said with purpose, and with some effort held his sword aloft.

After a second – during which I had the usual flicker of doubt wondering if he would really come – a peculiar chill descended around me. On feeling that chill my heart sped up with excitement. My eyes were wide open now, and I watched as a white and nebulous form slowly materialised before me, gradually taking the shape of a man. The obsidian ring on my finger began to grow hot and the white form took hold of the sword in its spectral hands. There was a sudden flash of light and heat that passed from the ring all the way down my hand and through my entire body.

I blinked slowly and when I opened my eyes Lieutenant Luke and I stood inches apart, his two strong hands over mine on the grip of his sword.

He is a man. He is a full, flesh and blood man.

I looked up into his handsome face and smiled broadly. 'Hi, Luke.'

'Good evening, Miss Pandora,' he said in his formal way, his hands still closed over mine. His bright blue eyes took in my face like a man who'd spent weeks in the desert would gaze upon a glass of water.

I grinned like an idiot.

Luke unburdened me of the sword and glanced briefly at the tall, arched windows. 'The moon is powerful tonight,' he remarked and slid his shining sabre into the metal sheath on the leather belt he wore around his waist.

'It is,' I replied.

Luke was dressed – as always – in the neatly pressed uniform of a Union soldier. It's what he'd been buried in and when he was a ghost, which was most of the time, that was how I saw him. In the flesh like this, the uniform was all the more striking. His dark blue cap was emblazoned with a pair of golden swords, crossed in the centre. Beneath it, his sandy blond hair was long around the collar. Luke had sideburns, which had been popular in his day. His 1860s frockcoat fitted his masculine form beautifully, the gleaming buttons done up all the way to the neck. The uniform was tailored at his broad shoulders and it tapered in at his slim waist, cinched tight with the leather belt. He had been a second lieutenant in the Lincoln Cavalry and had died in battle at the start of the Civil War when he was only twenty-five years old.

Somewhere along the way Luke's spirit had ended up trapped in this mansion in Spektor. He didn't really know why or how, and in our many discussions we'd talked about that mystery, and others, but on the night of the last full moon we'd discovered Luke's missing sword in a storage trunk in the mansion and that had been something of a breakthrough. It seemed his sword was a kind of talisman for him and although we didn't quite understand how it all worked yet, we guessed it was probably exhumed after his death by Dr Edmund Barrett, the paranormal scientist who apparently had considerable interest in raising the dead. Perhaps he'd been trying to communicate with Luke's spirit? Perhaps he'd been trying to divine the future? Whatever his intentions – and whether he knew what he'd done or not – it seemed Dr Barrett had cursed Luke's spirit to be trapped in the mansion he built.

And on that same night we'd also discovered that when the moon was full, my obsidian ring and Luke's sword appeared to act as amulets or talismans of some kind, allowing him to take human form again, if only for the night. That had been a rather pleasant revelation.

I could wait no longer. 'Thank you for coming,' I said and stretched up to circle my arms around his strong neck, marvelling at his solid form. I tilted my chin up, brought my mouth close to his, and when our lips finally met, flesh to flesh, I shut my eyes and felt a wave of pleasure and relief. Luke's mouth was warm and soft. I'd missed the sensation. Though my feet were firmly planted, as we kissed I felt like I was lifting from the floor. Luke had that effect on me.

Growing up, I'd always been able to communicate with spirits but never in my wildest fantasies had I imagined I would develop a crush on one.

'Tonight we're taking a walk,' I said after catching my breath. My face felt warm and I knew my cheeks were extra rosy. I slid my arms around Lieutenant Luke's firm waist.

He tilted his head. 'A walk?'

I nodded.

'Do you not wish to explore the mansion tonight?'

Since my great-aunt had given me the special skeleton key, we'd been doing a fair bit of that each night, when I was not too tired from my day job. The mansion had many undiscovered secrets and Celia had said that Luke was my 'spirit guide'. I didn't fully know what that term meant, but there was no denying he'd spent a lot of time in the mansion and knew it better than I did. We had been exploring it as a team.

'No,' I said. 'Tonight I just want to go on a normal date. I want to do the things normal people do.'

I nearly said 'things normal *couples* do', but that seemed a bit simplistic, perhaps even presumptuous. Our relationship was complicated. Luke was my friend, my spirit guide, my confidant and tonight he was my date. There was no need to complicate it with more labels.

'What sort of things do you wish to do, Miss Pandora?' Lieutenant Luke asked, and cupped my hand in his.

'I'll put my coat on and we'll find out.'

We stepped into the lounge room to find my great-aunt leaning against the doorway to the kitchen, resplendent in her emerald-green dress. From beneath the mesh of her veil she looked Luke up and down from head to toe and a slight smile crept across her pale features. She could not see him when he was in ghost form, but she could certainly see him now.

'Have fun,' she said, with what I thought was a touch of naughtiness in her voice. 'And remember, be back by midnight.'

There are many things that are only possible after dark. But night brings with it other concerns. And a need for precautions.

I was wearing Celia's warm vintage camel-coloured coat over my dress and had filled the pockets of the coat with handfuls of uncooked rice in case the residents who lived on the middle floors of the house decided to hassle us.

I stepped out of the elevator with Lieutenant Luke and we walked across the lobby of the great mansion hand in hand. I felt buoyant, if a little nervous, though I couldn't help but notice that my date's blue eyes (which did not glow when he was in human form but were nonetheless quite striking) appeared full of concern, his brows pulled together.

'Miss Pandora?' he said.

'Yes?'

'I do not want to disappoint you.'

'You could never disappoint me, Lieutenant Luke.'

We held hands tightly and walked across the tiles of the lobby. Under our feet were thin hairline cracks that ran the length of the beautifully tiled floor, as if the house had survived some mild earthquake or its foundations sat near a fault line, and it made me think again about the strange noises I had heard.

'Do you ever hear strange noises in the house?' I found myself asking.

Luke nodded.

'I mean, down here? Noises that seem like they're coming from under the floor?'

He nodded again. 'The house has many things to tell us.'

So it wasn't just me.

Let's just have a nice date tonight, I reminded myself once again. Like two normal people on a normal date. Two normal people with a bit of a generation gap.

I was nervous about something, I realised. Maybe it was this next bit – leaving the house – or maybe it was something else entirely.

'Here we go ...'

I reached for the door with my right hand and Lieutenant Luke immediately let go of my left. *Oh boy.* I plastered a big smile on my face to hide my nerves.

We'd been on the roof of the house one month earlier, when it was a full moon and he was in human form as he was tonight, and the roof was technically outside the building, right? Still, this next bit was something I was a little uncertain about. And it seemed Luke was uncertain, too. We'd tried this once before when he was in spirit form. It had not gone well. But this would be different, wouldn't it?

Still smiling, I turned the doorknob, pushed the front door open and stepped out into the cool spring night. I held the door open with one hand and held my other hand out to Luke.

'Come with me,' I said.

He stood stiffly in his uniform, handsome and intoxicatingly real, the sheathed sword hanging from his belt.

Trust me to have a crush on a ghost.

Who else would have a date they might not be able to leave the house with, for, um, technical reasons?

'You can do it. You're flesh and blood tonight,' I reasoned.

Finally Luke closed his eyes and took a few steps forward. I realised I was holding my breath as he neared the threshold, one step at a time. The last time we'd tried this, he'd disappeared. But we did not have his sword then. Or this powerful moon and its magick. He had not been in human form. This had to be different. This had to work.

Come on ...

Lieutenant Luke stepped right up to the doorway

and stopped. He lifted his left foot just a touch, his boot hovering near the threshold.

Oh, Luke . . .

He closed his eyes but mine were wide open. This was it. This was the difference between whether or not we would ever be able to leave the house together, whether he would ever be able to walk the streets of Spektor, Manhattan, the world even. Whether he could ever be part of the other aspects of my life, beyond the walls of this strange old house . . .

I watched him move as if in slow motion, waiting for him to dematerialise, but his foot came down on the other side. He stepped through the doorway and stood in front of me, a peculiar look on his face. 'I'm out,' he remarked, not quite believing it.

He was out. He was.

We linked arms and I took a deep breath. 'Good,' I said, trying to sound casual. 'Now, let's see Manhattan.'

CHAPTER
THREE

$\mathcal{I}$t was a beautiful, clear spring night as I stood on the observation deck of the Empire State Building, eighty-six storeys above Manhattan, holding hands with my lovely, temporarily undeceased date.

All around us the city's famous skyscrapers glowed from within, illuminating the sky with thousands of cubes of light. Below us a wide grid of streets stretched off in all directions, alive with taxis and cars, pedestrians and movement, flashing billboards and neon lights. In the distance, Lady Liberty held her torch aloft and, above her, a spectacular Crow Moon sat low and full in the sky, bringing her ancient, otherworldly presence to the modern urban dreamscape. In that moment I had to admit to myself that while my new life in New York was not at all as I'd imagined, there was no denying that it was tremendously exciting.

Scary, too, at times.

There had been moments in the previous three months when I'd truly wondered if I would cope – if I would survive, even. There were things in this world that I'd only read about in folktales and fiction. I'd seen proof of things that even the most open-minded person would reject as fanciful. There was a lot to get my head around. What would my parents make of what I was doing now, for instance? Holding the hand of a dead Civil War soldier who'd never seen modern Manhattan, and who had come to life for the night thanks to a trick of a talisman and the magick of the moon?

Yet even though my new life was strange and challenging, I could see that I finally belonged somewhere. I had a sense of acceptance that I'd missed since losing my parents. It was almost as if I'd just been waiting in Gretchenville for the past eight years, biding my time until Manhattan summoned me.

'Miss Pandora, there is so much life,' Lieutenant Luke said in a hushed voice

The Empire State Building opened in 1931, some seventy years after Lieutenant Luke's death, so naturally this was his first time on the observation platform of the famous building. Now, as I turned my head to take in his expression, I could see that he was quite mesmerised by the view of the contemporary metropolis. His strong jaw had softened somehow with his awe, and those eyes of his – the most incredible blue eyes you'll ever see – were fixed brightly on our surroundings.

'There is,' I replied simply. 'There is.'

He squeezed my hand.

Luke is a true gentleman in the old-fashioned sense, and he is also the one person in the world – correction: *worlds* – that I knew would enjoy the delights of the

Empire State Building with the same childlike wonder I did. Just like me, he had had something of a limited experience of the world until recently. I guess we had that much in common, if not much else. I could not imagine dying in a war, leaving behind a spouse and unborn baby. (His pregnant wife had been my age, he'd told me.) Or finding myself trapped in a house as a spirit that most people could never see and would never recognise or acknowledge, not knowing why I was there, not even knowing how it had happened. What loneliness that fate must hold. I leaned my head into Luke's chest and he circled his arms around me. Yes, we'd both had our losses.

'This building is said to have many ghosts. I met one named Evelyn McHale. She's nice, if sad,' I said, wondering why I couldn't resist talking to a ghost about ghosts, as if it would interest him. Or perhaps telling Luke about others like him would make him feel less alone?

'There's something called the "Automotive Bermuda Triangle",' I went on as Luke continued to gaze out at the city. 'The so-called "Empire State Building Effect". Apparently, about a dozen automobiles are disabled within a five-block radius of this building every day. They just stop working or once they've been parked they won't start again.' I'd read about the phenomenon with some fascination.

'I do not know how these automotive carriages work. I have never been inside one, myself,' Lieutenant Luke remarked, considering the idea.

Automotive carriages. That was another experience for our list, then.

'But I would not care to ride a horse that halted when I needed him to canter,' he continued. 'Such behaviour could be dangerous for the rider.'

I turned and smiled. 'Indeed. Well, this is unusual activity. Cars are usually a bit more reliable than that. More reliable than horses,' I said.

'More reliable than a good horse?'

Lieutenant Luke would have been quite a horseman in his day, I reminded myself. 'Maybe a good horse is very reliable, but cars are usually pretty safe, unless you have a real lemon on your hands.'

From his expression I realised that he didn't understand what I meant. 'A lemon is a poor quality car,' I said. Of course he wasn't familiar with modern slang. 'One theory says the big antenna on top of the building causes this Bermuda Triangle effect. It's a radio and television antenna and they think it interferes with the electrics.' I looked above us and Luke followed my eye line. 'Or maybe it's something else,' I said, thinking of the jumpers like Evelyn and the workers who had died during the construction. Industry estimates at the time stated that one death per floor of construction was to be expected but, thankfully, many reports put the final toll at far fewer than that.

'What do you think it is that causes this "triangle" you speak of?' he asked.

I shrugged. New York held many mysteries. We knew that better than most. 'I don't know,' I said. 'I'd believe just about anything at this point.'

We looked out over the city in silence.

'Can we stay a while longer?' Lieutenant Luke asked. I nodded and he put his arms around my waist again, and we watched the world together for a blissful stretch of time that might have been twenty minutes or an hour, I couldn't say. It seemed like we'd developed such a connection that we understood each other without even speaking. I could feel him within me. It was a closeness I found foreign and intoxicating, and I felt truly happy there, with Luke's arms linked around my waist. We watched the planes traverse the giant night sky, the cars moving below. The city pulse. The moon. I didn't even see any of the ghosts said to inhabit the place. It felt almost *normal*. It was perfect.

And then it all had to change.

The doors opened directly behind us in a rush of moving air and, naturally, we both turned. And there he was.

Jay Rockwell.

He stepped out onto the breezy platform not three feet from where Lieutenant Luke and I stood. Jay was an athletic six foot six with an impressive physique formed from years of competitive rowing in college. He was wearing jeans and his familiar leather jacket, with a woolly scarf wrapped loosely around his neck. He had a full head of dark brown, close-cropped hair and what is commonly called 'ruggedly handsome' good looks. On spotting his face I immediately blurted a greeting.

'Oh, hi, Jay!'

And as soon as I did I found myself caught in one of those awkward moments. You know, the moment when your dead boyfriend meets your ex-boyfriend-with-amnesia-who-doesn't-remember-you.

Jay jerked his head around to look at us. 'Uh, hi ...' he said. 'Do I know you?'

I blanched. Luke and I let go of each other and stood side by side. My date was dead silent.

Of course Jay Rockwell didn't remember me. I'd known that but I'd forgotten it for just long enough to make a fool of myself. He was one of the more charming (living) men I'd met in my life. We'd dated briefly, but he didn't remember anything of it since a four-hundred-year-old entrepreneur named Elizabeth Bathory attacked us. Because Jay wasn't the target − I was − he'd been 'erased'. That was how the supernatural world dealt with the little issue of confidentiality. By giving guys like Jay Rockwell amnesia so they wouldn't go around declaring the presence of ... well, everything you can imagine and more. Ghosts, zombies, witches, vampires ... I mean, *Sanguine*. The existence of Sanguine.

'Um ...' was all that came out as I tried to think of what to say.

I couldn't tell Jay Rockwell that I'd saved him from a gang of ill-tempered women with fangs and a thirst for mischief and human blood. That wasn't going to work at all.

'I think we met at ...' I stopped. I tried again. 'We, uh ...'

Oh, I'm a terrible liar.

'I work for *Pandora* magazine,' I finally managed. 'My name is Pandora English.'

'Oh. Pandora?' Jay replied, seeming not to recall

either myself or the magazine, but trying to cover it, trying to be smooth.

Just then a woman appeared. I could tell she was Jay's date because she was very, very beautiful, and she arrived in a short dress and a cloud of expensive cosmetics to latch onto his arm with that air of protectiveness some women have around their dates. *So, they haven't been dating long*, I thought, a bit surprised at my own jealousy.

The woman was about twenty-five, the same age as Jay (and the same age as Luke, if you didn't count the hundred and fifty years of dead time). She smiled glowingly at Jay and then looked at Luke and I with amusement. 'You two been to a costume party?' she asked.

I coughed.

Luke was wearing his uniform, of course. He didn't have much choice about that. If he wasn't near the cavalry sword he wore around his waist he simply dissolved into his ghostly form again, and I doubted he could even escape the house like that. Yes, it was a relief that Luke was finally able to venture from the mansion walls in his human body when the moon was full and 'the magick high', as my great-aunt put it. But he was still in that uniform, sword and all.

He did stand out a touch.

'Greetings,' Lieutenant Luke finally offered. 'Ma'am, I am dressed in this uniform for a special party, as you say,' he said stiffly.

Hearing his voice aloud in front of other people made my head swim.

Jay's date burst out laughing. 'Oh, that's so good! You really sound old-worldy.' She turned to me. 'And what are you going as, some kind of secretary?'

My smile was so big and so fake it could have snapped off like an icicle.

'This dress belonged to Lauren Bacall, as a matter of fact,' I retorted after a beat, pulling the edges of my coat back a touch to show it off. The sapphire dress fluttered in the wind.

'You look very beautiful,' Jay told me sincerely, but unwisely.

Jay's date shot him a look. I noticed Luke tense a little.

'I took my blonde wig off,' I continued. 'It was getting itchy.'

I was not as glamorous as Bacall and I can't imagine I looked dressed up for a costume party, but never mind. If Jay and his date had any idea they were talking to a woman with some strange 'gifts' and man who'd died in the Civil War, they didn't let on.

'Have a good time. It was nice to see you again, uh ...'

'Pandora,' I said. 'And you, too, Jay. I hope everything is going well at *Men Only Magazine*.' I didn't much approve of the magazine he worked for. I thought it was a bit heavy on ladies airbrushed into small bathers and a bit light on what you'd call content. Not that it mattered as he didn't even remember me. But that was fine.

Yup, that was fine.

We all exchanged smiles. Mine, I'm sure, was a little strained. Then Jay and his date wandered off to another part of the observation deck.

In the late 1940s the edge of the observation platform had been fenced in with a tall, wire barrier, and now I stepped up to the mesh and closed my fingers around it, feeling the wind blowing back my hair and pushing the hem of my dress flat against my knees. I looked out over the city, feeling unsettled. Perhaps it was inevitable that leaving the house with Luke would be awkward at some point, but what were the chances of running into Jay, of all people? Perhaps I shouldn't have been so ambitious. Perhaps a stroll through Central Park, where we were less likely to run into people, would have been wiser, especially for our first time out together.

'Are you well, Miss Pandora?' Lieutenant Luke asked. He touched my elbow gently.

I nodded, still staring out over the city.

We took the lift back down to ground level without saying a word, and when we stepped out onto the street we saw that Jay and his haughty date had linked arms and were walking away from the building. Jay's outrageously expensive, low-slung silver Ferrari was parked nearby. I'd recognise it anywhere. I'd had a bit of trouble getting into that car in a knee-length dress with a split, so I couldn't imagine how his date would negotiate it in her skimpy outfit.

Stop it, I thought.

I wondered if his car would start, or if they'd be a victim of the Empire State Building Effect.

Stop!

I pulled my gaze away.

The walk home with Lieutenant Luke was quieter than I'd hoped. It wasn't like we were purposely not talking. It was more like something was on both our minds and neither of us were ready to air our thoughts just yet.

Central Park was lit only by the occasional lamp post, and the cover of darkness was a comforting camouflage after the public exposure of the Empire State Building. At this hour the park felt uninhabited, except for the odd set of joggers. Few New Yorkers dared to traverse this area alone at night, and that badly timed observation brought me back to memories of Jay driving me home from our date only a couple of months earlier — a date he had no recollection of.

'You find him attractive,' Lieutenant Luke said suddenly, and I was pulled out of my thoughts as effectively as if smelling salts had been put under my nose.

Oh boy. There was little doubt of whom he spoke.

'Jay is ... well ...' I stopped next to a bench. 'Jay helped me get to know New York a bit. He was nice to me.'

Jay Rockwell and I had found ourselves in the same elevator together and, later, at a party for the beauty cream *BloodofYouth* (now discontinued). Jay had been one of the first people I'd met in Manhattan and he'd taken me on my first 'proper' date, ever. I recalled how he'd driven me home through this very park in his Ferrari, and remarked that I ought not be so silly as to venture through the park at night by myself. At the time, I'd taken some serious offence at his patronising comment. It had seemed a cruel reference to my humble, small-town upbringing. Yet now I did exactly that most evenings after work. Walking through Central Park was simply the quickest way home from the subway station at 103rd Street in Spanish Harlem. Rightly or wrongly, after everything else I'd seen, the common dangers of Central Park seemed relatively insignificant. And though things hadn't got particularly serious between Jay and me – Jay's memory had been erased before things could get serious – I'd probably always have a soft spot for him. Even if he didn't remember me.

And things *couldn't* get serious with Luke, because he was not really human. That was the real issue here, wasn't it?

'Yes, Jay is an attractive man,' I said honestly. I couldn't lie to Luke. 'And you are very handsome. But you and he are very different. Jay doesn't know me like you do. In fact, he doesn't know me at all, as you may have noticed.'

I watched Luke's beautiful face. He did seem a bit sensitive about being dead.

'Can we sit for a moment?' I asked and took a seat on one end of the park bench. Luke sat next to me as I'd suggested, though I noticed we weren't touching.

'Are you okay, Miss Pandora? Are your feet tired? I can carry you,' he offered. We had walked quite a distance from West 34th to here.

I shook my head. 'I'm fine,' I said, though the thought was rather appealing. Luke was strong enough to sweep me up effortlessly. He'd done it before.

'May I take your hand?' he asked.

I nodded. 'Yes.'

Lieutenant Luke took my hand in both of his and looked me in the eyes. 'Miss Pandora, I am your spirit guide. Perhaps ...'

We hadn't had this conversation before but, of course, it was coming. The obvious questions. Could Luke and I really be more than friends? Could a romance between us be anything but doomed, when I was nineteen and he was twenty-five plus one hundred and fifty years? The gaps in age and mortality were an issue. Weren't they?

'You are alive. You must enjoy everything of life,' he said earnestly. 'It would not be right for me to hold you back. It is natural if you want to spend time with Jay. It is normal that you should want to be in the company of living men, like him.'

'Shhh,' I said, and held a finger to Luke's lovely mouth. I couldn't handle this relationship talk. Not right now. I'd waited all month for this date, and I just couldn't believe Jay had walked into the middle of it.

'Let's not talk about all this right now—'

Suddenly Luke jerked his head away, as if hearing something in the distance that I could not detect with my ears. When he finally turned back to face me, I saw a flicker of serious concern in his eyes. 'Miss Pandora, there is a strong presence in the mansion,' he said gravely, appearing to concentrate on that thing I could not hear or see.

I sat a little straighter on the bench. 'What kind of presence?' I asked. 'My boss Skye again?'

Lieutenant Luke had alerted me to Skye's apparent visits to Spektor. It seemed likely she'd been summoned by Athanasia, whom I hadn't seen for a while.

'Or has Athanasia risen?' I asked nervously.

She was Sanguine. And she'd tried to eat me. At the thought of her I pulled my collar up higher on my neck.

'No. Neither of them,' Luke said. 'This is something very powerful.' His chiselled jaw clenched.

'Celia's friend Deus?' I asked, but Luke did not answer.

He appeared to glaze over, looking back in the direction of the house.

'Are you okay?' I was becoming concerned.

'Miss Pandora, something is not right,' he managed in a strained voice. He did not look at me.

And then he stood suddenly, as rigid as a statue.

'Luke?'

I leapt off the bench and stood in front of him. Lieutenant Luke looked right through me, his gaze fixed on something in the distance. Was his face turning … pale? 'What is it? What's going on?'

He didn't answer.

Was he turning white? My goddess, he was. 'Luke, what's happening?'

I reached for him and to my horror my hand went straight through his. I tried again and both of my arms passed through him. I glanced anxiously around but could see nothing or no one that could be causing his reversion to ghost form. And we were still in Central Park and nowhere near the mansion. Was anyone seeing this?

'Luke!' I cried.

It was no use. In seconds there was nothing left of him.

Luke was gone, his cavalry sword on the grass at my feet.

CHAPTER
FOUR

T jogged the rest of the way through Central Park in my flats, carrying Lieutenant Luke's sword. I was alone in the park far later than usual – it was nearly eleven o'clock – but I figured any nefarious types would think twice about messing with me with a gleaming blade in my hand.

By the time I hit the little tunnel that led to Spektor I was winded and working hard to keep myself from freaking out. I emerged onto Addams Avenue clinging to the hope that Luke would be there, even in ghost form, waiting for me just beyond the mist.

He was not.

I stopped on the edge of Addams Avenue and caught my breath. Strange clusters of fog drifted like tumbleweeds across the dark street, seeming in turns to grow arms and legs, to walk on ghostly feet, before dissolving into mist again. Faint, flickering lights could be seen in the windows of a few of the old brownstones. Harold's Grocer was open, as always, lights burning brightly, and as I passed the old-fashioned sign at the front I thought fleetingly of going inside and asking for Harold's help. But what could he do?

Looking ahead, I thought I saw a couple of figures, just outside the mansion. I squinted. I hoped one might be Luke.

Oh dear.

No. Not Luke. Not Celia. I recognised the figures ahead as a couple of local Spektorites known only to me as Blonde and Redhead. The former wore a hot-pink leather minidress that showed off her enviable long legs and arms, and the latter wore a black pencil skirt with a cinched satin bustier. Both were loaded with enough designer costume jewellery to make Madonna jealous and neither wore coats, despite the crisp spring night air. Blonde and Redhead were ridiculously attractive, as you would expect of those who get paid to model things for a living. Well, not for a *living* per se, but their looks could sell ice cubes to Arctic explorers. At a glance you would swear they were two of the most gorgeous, if underdressed, people you'd ever seen. But I knew better. These two were what was left of an undead pack of supermodels, led by Athanasia, my nemesis.

Athanasia, their leader, had 'gone to ground' to heal after an incident involving some garlic bread I had hand-delivered to her face.

Their kind were Sanguine. Vampires to use the politically incorrect term, which in this case was awfully tempting. The existence of the Sanguine was not well known. The Sanguine community saw to that by removing human witnesses, or at least the memories of those witnesses – a policy that brought its own complications – complications like erasing Jay Rockwell's memory. These two were not very nice, though they certainly had been pretty popular during the New York fashion scene's so-called vampire chic trend a few months ago (now uncool again), not that any of the photographers and designers who'd hired them had any idea their vampirically pale skin was vampiric for the obvious reason.

Hmmm.

My great-aunt Celia had a peculiar agreement with the powerful Sanguine known as Deus – the one I'd have to face at midnight – and that agreement involved allowing the unused floors of the mansion to be available as a kind of halfway house for wayward vamps, hence the boarded-up windows. It was not an ideal arrangement for me, as a warm-blooded breather, but it was her house and her rules and that was that. She had to have her reasons. Though most of the Sanguine I'd met did not exactly impress me – actually, they positively terrified me – I had met a couple who weren't so bad. One, Samantha, was almost a friend. Almost. I mean, how good a friend can someone be if you're never really sure they won't try to neck you? And Deus was terrifying but he seemed kind of reasonable. But there was little that was reasonable about these two women and their leader Athanasia. They didn't play well with others and they really had a problem with me. I'd staked Athanasia (unsuccessfully ... oops) and that was even before the garlic bread incident. In fact, the only thing stopping these two from attacking me right now was Celia's protection as mistress of the house. Anyone who laid a hand on me risked eviction and I guess there weren't too many places like Celia's around, so these two weren't keen to leave their cosy accommodations.

Nonetheless, they sure enjoyed taunting me.

'Well, if it isn't Miss Country,' Blonde said, sneering as I approached. She posed in her mini as I passed her, jutting out one hip. The leather squeaked a little. Maybe it was Pleather.

'Look at her. She's so pathetic,' Redhead said.

I need to find Luke and I don't have time for this, I thought.

I tried to pass her to reach the front door but Redhead blocked me and I instinctively raised the tip of Luke's sword a touch. She stood proud and defiant, her pale, flawless hands on the tiny waist of her cinched bustier, ivory fangs blatantly hanging over her painted lips. She clearly didn't feel like getting out of my way, sword or no sword.

She looks hungry, I thought uneasily, glancing at those fangs.

'What do you want?' I said.

'When Athanasia gets back, you're history,' she warned me, bending down to speak right into my face. Her breath smelled like a butcher's shop. Then she poked my shoulder hard. Her manicure was pretty, but sharp.

'Yeah. She's gonna rip your throat out!' Blonde chimed in, moving closer. They were now on either side of me.

'I'm sure that will be just lovely,' I said, trying to keep the situation under control. 'But in the meantime I was wondering if you could tell me if you saw a man in a uniform pass by here? I'm looking for him.'

Even before they replied I could see from their faces that they hadn't seen Lieutenant Luke, which was disappointing. Then again he had reverted from his human form and the undead, like most of the living, did not generally see ghosts.

'Thanks anyway,' I said, hopeful that Luke was already in the house. I tried to continue past Redhead, holding the sword ahead of me.

'Bet you don't even know how to use that thing,' she said, taking a deliberate step to block me again. 'You stupid cow.'

It's not worth it, I reminded myself.

'Ha ha ha. Cow! She does look a bit bovine. Or like a fat little piggy. Oink, oink. Little *morchilla*,' Blonde taunted.

Morchilla. Blood sausage.

Not. Worth. It.

I really didn't need this kind of hassle, not now. I knew I should ignore them. I was not fat, or farm-animal-like, though admittedly, sometimes I was a little insecure about hailing from Gretchenville. They were just running through insults to see which ones would stick and I supposed if they'd planned to kill me and risk being thrown out of the mansion they would have done it already. I gritted my teeth, wishing they'd just finish their taunts and let me pass. What if Lieutenant Luke needed me? I had his sword, which should surely give Sanguine some pause, shouldn't it? I mean, wasn't it Celia who'd explained that stakes were only for holding vampires down while you beheaded them? In my experience, Celia was never wrong, and the kind of blade I was holding could surely be an instrument for head cleaving, if you were into that sort of thing. Yuck, but still ... Life or un-death, right? Both of them had sharp fangs hanging out of their pretty faces and things were not looking good for me. As Fledglings, their impulses could spiral out of control.

At least my pockets weren't empty.

I slid my left hand into the pocket of my coat. 'Oh, oops,' I said, and pulled out a handful of uncooked white rice. The grains hit the steps outside the mansion with a shimmering bounce. Immediately, Redhead's eyes were averted by the movement. She got down on her knees.

'Oh! One, two, three, four, five ...'

Seconds later Blonde was also on her knees. 'One, two ...'

Fledgling Sanguine had an obsessive compulsive need to count, which had led to the centuries-old – and wise – belief that scattering seeds or rice in graveyards and outside homes slowed the progress of the undead. I suppose that legend was where Sesame Street's Count von Count came from. In some versions of the folktale, Sanguine counted a single grain per year but, sadly, that wasn't the reality. Fledgling Sanguine counted pretty quickly – rice, pumpkin seeds, carrot seeds, poppy seeds, millet, sand – but still they counted. Until they grew out of the habit, that is, which, lucky for me, these two clearly had not.

By the time they'd counted to ten, I was inside the mansion. The lights were off – Blonde and Redhead were probably being energy-efficient – and I had to grope around on the wall to find the switch for the chandelier. Once it was on and I could see I was alone, I moved across the lobby with haste, got in the lift and pressed the button for the penthouse, wondering when and if Athanasia would return.

Mostly though, I hoped Lieutenant Luke was okay, and that he was in the house somewhere. Our date could hardly have been more disastrous and I couldn't help but feel responsible.

At half past eleven I knocked and entered my great-aunt's penthouse. Once inside the safety of those walls I stopped, leaned against the door and felt a blue mood descend over me like a fisherman's net. I didn't even sing out my usual greeting.

My great-aunt still had the curtains pulled open in the large lounge room and I could see the full moon and the faint dots of blinking constellations above the Empire State Building beyond the veil of Spektor's eternal fog. Somehow the stars always looked brighter here, despite the fog.

Celia was in her reading nook and she peered around the corner, registered my expression and said, 'You need a cup of tea.'

Always the tea.

She walked into the kitchen, Freyja trailing behind

her. I slipped my flats off and noticed for the first time that I had earned some fresh blisters from all the walking and running across the city. Hanging my head, I watched Celia put the kettle on, her every movement calm and practised. Freyja purred against my ankles, her albino fur feeling soft and warm. She sat down at my feet and stared intensely at my hand with her large, opal eyes. She meowed. Her tail twitched.

She was staring at Luke's sword.

I should try, I thought.

'I'll be with you in just a moment,' I said, and ducked back into the lounge room.

'Take your time, darling,' my great-aunt called back.

I stepped up to the arched windows to stand directly in the moonlight, uncertain about whether or not that would make a scrap of difference. Spektor was quiet outside, and only the sound of the boiling kettle broke the silence of the house. I took a few deep breaths and tried to centre myself. *You can do it. You can.* Eyes closed, I lifted Lieutenant Luke's cavalry sword into the air and said his name with purpose. Seconds passed. I tried to concentrate, tried to feel his arrival, but there was nothing. No chill in the air. No Luke. My ring did not warm up or flash with heat.

'Lieutenant Luke,' I declared again, pointing the heavy sword towards the moon. I took another deep breath. 'Luke?' His name choked in my throat.

Finally I lowered my arm and when I opened my eyes I saw that Freyja had followed me out of the kitchen and was looking at me strangely. Celia was still preparing her tea, seemingly unperturbed by my failed ritual. Actually, she always seemed unperturbed. There was a high-pitched whine as the kettle boiled, and when I joined her again she was engaged in the task of filling a beautiful antique teapot, steam rising up around her. I watched her from the doorway, my shoulders hunched. The penthouse had filled with the rich scent of fragrant tea leaves.

'He's not coming when he's called, is he?' Celia remarked without turning.

I nodded to myself, feeling a sting in my eyes. 'You haven't seen him, have you?'

'No. I haven't seen your soldier since you two left.' She shook her head, the widow's veil shifting on her perfectly coiffed black hair.

I placed Luke's sword lovingly on the round kitchen table. Where could he be? What had called him? What had happened to his human form? Was he a spirit again? If so, why would he not communicate? Since my first night in Spektor we'd been in regular contact. He'd said I could call on him anytime, and I'd soon realised that he meant it. It's true, we did not communicate every night, but he'd never once failed to arrive when I'd asked for him.

Perhaps I'd taken that for granted.

I folded my arms over my chest, realising my coat was still on. 'I'll hang this up.'

My great-aunt approached me with a cup of tea. 'Drink,' she said. 'You will feel better.'

I took the cup and saucer, and sat down on her leather hassock. I sipped once. Twice. It was rejuvenating.

'Deus will be here soon, and you shall speak with him,' she said.

'Do you think he'll know what happened to Luke? He just ... disappeared when we were in Central Park.'

'I am not sure.'

These weren't words my great-aunt used often.

'Before he ... disappeared,' I said, my heart constricting with the words, 'Luke told me there was a powerful force here at the house.'

'Oh yes,' she said, unsurprised. 'There is indeed a powerful force here. Oh, and don't forget to tell Deus about the trouble you are having with those two friends of Athanasia's.'

She knows about that?

'Of course I know,' she said.

CHAPTER
FIVE

$\mathcal{B}$y the time midnight loomed I still had not found Lieutenant Luke.

I'd tried to summon him several times using his cavalry sword, finally tiring out my right arm to the point where I wondered if I'd even be able to raise a glass of water. Eventually I placed his heavy sword across the top of the antique writing desk in my room on its soft velvet cloth, where it sat under the open windows, shining in the moonlight.

I stared at it, feeling empty inside.

There was no way I could bear to put it away under the bed. Not yet.

All that excruciating anticipation. And disappointment. Where had we gone wrong, exactly? It had all happened so fast. Was there some sort of time limit on Luke's ability to escape the mansion walls? I had no idea. I had to work at *Pandora* in the morning and I didn't know if I could go to sleep yet – or if I'd be able to at all, worrying as I was about Luke – but regardless, there was one more thing left to do, and that thing gave me little comfort.

I emerged from my room at midnight sharp, wearing my good jeans and my best vintage blouse. It was time to meet with the ancient Sanguine.

Deus.

Celia had already fixed a fresh pot of tea and arranged it neatly on her silver tray. She handed it to me and I looked down at the two cups – one for me, and one for her undead friend – and I felt a little afraid.

'Thanks,' I said quietly.

I carried the tray as Celia led me down the hall to her end of the penthouse, my right arm shaking a little. For the first couple of months that I'd lived here, this end of the penthouse had been strictly forbidden territory. My great-aunt liked her privacy. I totally understood that. But I suspected she'd also been wanting to protect me after I'd first arrived, because now that I was more aware of the potential dangers in the house she'd given me her blessing to investigate its secrets – in particular, the hidden corridors and stairwells that snaked through this end of the building. The architect Dr Barrett had a laboratory in the lower floors somewhere, and he'd made it hard to find so that he wasn't disturbed while he was working. Barrett had been into some dark stuff, it seemed. Necromancy and who knew what else. Celia had, however, been quite firm that I was absolutely, *under no circumstances*, to venture *below* the basement. So far, I hadn't even found the basement, Barrett's laboratory, or let alone anything lower.

The room where I was meeting Deus was a special, sunken chamber just beyond the main hallway, and it suited our meeting because it was separate from the rest of the penthouse. No Sanguine could venture into the main penthouse. (Which seemed like an awfully good rule as far as I was concerned.) The skeleton key did fit the lock of this door, but I didn't need it tonight. The door was unlocked and Celia pushed it open for me with one pale hand and gave me an encouraging pat on the shoulder with the other, urging me inside.

'Good luck.'

I took a breath and made my way down the three stone steps, balancing the tray, before Celia closed the door behind me. *Oh boy*, I thought as the door shut. I was more than a little nervous about seeing Deus again, especially considering the circumstances of our last meeting.

He hadn't arrived yet, I noted, but he would soon enough. He wasn't the type to be late.

In part because he could fly.

Oh boy.

The antechamber was candlelit and it smelled pleasantly of frankincense. Carved wooden furniture decorated the space, along with heavy velvet drapes that hung over the stone walls, suspended from ornate iron rods. A velvet chaise longue. Persian rugs. The effect was luxurious and intimate, if dark. It spoke of another time, somehow even older than the uniquely Victorian feel of the rest of the house, though it seemed unlikely that it could have been built before 1880. I noticed that Celia had lit the three special candles of different colours that I recalled having seen before, an offering to the 'Triple Goddess' – the Maiden, Mother and Crone.

I placed the silver tray with its tea fixings on the low, circular table in the centre of the chamber. After a moment I took my place on the burgundy velvet seat of one of the two ornate wooden chairs. While I waited, I looked around, trying to calm my anxiousness about Luke and about Deus, and prepare myself for what was to come. My eyes continually wandered back to the chaise longue, which I'd woken on, after being rescued by Deus under the last full moon.

And my eyes went again and again to the full-sized coffin in the corner.

It will be fine. It will all be fine, I told myself, though my mouth was dry.

Thankfully the wait was not too long. After a minute I heard faint footsteps below me. Then there came the knock.

'Um, come in,' I said in an exaggerated voice, and the casket creaked. A single smooth hand pushed the lid open, fingers curled around the edge. Slowly, my visitor revealed himself, rising up from the base of the coffin inch by inch, giving me a little shiver. The creature who emerged was a couple of inches taller than me – perhaps five foot nine or so – and he was about as far from a rotting corpse as one could imagine. In fact, he looked rather chic in a slim-fitting dark suit and white, crisp shirt, the collar sitting high on his neck. His skin was darker than you might expect of someone who'd been dead for so long. His eyebrows were dark and dramatic, his eyelashes inky black and distractingly long.

And he was smiling.

Deus.

'Good evening, Pandora English,' he said in his curiously attractive accent.

'Good evening, Deus,' I replied, panicking a little inside.

That smile.

Deus was a Kathakano – the traditional Sanguine of ancient Crete. The Kathakano always smile. That trait was peculiar to their race and I fully suspected those Kathakano smiles had deceived many an unwary victim over the centuries. As a member of one of the oldest race of Sanguine in the world (perhaps even the oldest?), Deus was undeniably powerful. As a rule, the older a Sanguine is, the more power, skills and 'trickery' they have mastered, and the more magnetic they are. Deus had no weakness for counting rice, that was for certain. In fact, I found it hard to imagine he had any weaknesses at all.

'Thank you for meeting with me.'

'Of course,' I said. 'Please take a seat.' My voice sounded level. I was proud of that.

He lowered himself into the chair opposite me, as smooth as water.

'Tea?' I offered.

He folded one leg over the other. 'That would be most kind. Thank you,' he said.

I poured him a cup, irritated that my strained right arm was not as steady as my voice had been. I didn't bother with the jug of milk. Deus was lactose intolerant, I knew. He accepted his cup with a courteous nod.

Those eyelashes. They are so long. Look at them. He was still grinning, of course, and I smiled back, a bit flushed. I reminded myself that it took a certain level of conscious concentration to avoid staring at him. It wasn't because he was so beautiful. He wasn't, really. It was his natural, predatory effect at work, that was all. Celia had assured me that I'd grow used to it in time, that I'd eventually find it a little easier to resist. But so far this evening it felt harder, not easier.

I poured myself a cup of tea and took a sip. I swallowed. 'Do you know where Luke is? Did you do something to him?' I managed.

Deus was sipping his tea, and now he paused and gave me a curious look. 'The soldier?'

'Yes. My friend Second Lieutenant Luke Thomas,' I said. 'He disappeared tonight.'

'Isn't that common?'

Very funny.

'I was with him in Central Park and he disappeared. I can't find him,' I explained, though it was already fairly clear that Deus did not know about the situation and was unlikely to be able to help me with it.

'I have no dominion over his kind, Pandora English. He is departed. That is rather more your department.'

I frowned. Was that true? Perhaps it was. There was certainly a big difference between dead and undead.

'Will you please keep your eyes open, in case ...' I trailed off. Deus could not see Luke's ghost. Neither could Celia. How could they help me find Luke? 'Never mind,' I said, holding my cup of tea and saucer in my lap. I looked at the cup, considering what to say. 'What I mean is . . . just, if you hear anything about him, will you please let me know?'

'Absolutely,' Deus replied, smiling, and I kind of believed him. So far I'd found him to be fairly honest. That didn't seem like a typical trait for the Sanguine, but perhaps deceptiveness was like arithmomania and it was something Deus had learned to master over the centuries. Like flight.

His ability to fly was precisely how he'd saved me from falling several storeys to my death – a fact that made me deeply uncomfortable. So was the realisation that I was staring at him again.

His skin. It's so luminous. So . . .

'I have come to warn you,' he said abruptly.

I tore my gaze from his features again. 'Go on,' I said.

He unfolded his legs and placed his tea on the tray. 'Pandora English, you need to be aware that there is a powerful force in Spektor.'

'A powerful force.' Luke had said the very same thing before he disappeared, but it was especially alarming to hear someone as powerful as Deus talk of 'powerful' forces. 'What does that mean exactly?'

'There is a powerful force here. Something new. Beyond that, I cannot say,' he replied, much to my frustration.

'Cannot or *will not?*'

It was then I could tell that his effect on me was wearing off a bit. I was becoming more confident in his presence. Deus seemed to sense it, too. He smiled more broadly.

'What kind of force? Do you mean like the spider goddess?' I didn't think I could survive another encounter like that.

'There have been no sightings of that nature, thankfully. The spider is still well?'

I nodded. She was being kept safely in Celia's lounge room in her little cage, reduced to life as a normal black widow. 'Thank you, by the way, for ...'

'Naturally,' Deus said, and waved his hand, as if saving me had been nothing. No human could have been quick enough. No human could have done what he had.

'There is no debt. You did save Spektor,' he said. 'So, in a way, you'd saved my life already. You'd saved all of us.'

I did, didn't I? That was still a bit hard to comprehend. But I truly hoped that Deus meant what he said about me not being indebted to him.

'So you have come to warn me that there is a powerful force in Spektor, but you can't or won't tell me what it is?'

His eyes glinted at me, that eternal smile unfaltering. I leaned back in my seat.

'I come to you with a warning, Pandora. The time is approaching.'

'The time? What do you mean, "the time"? You mean the revolution?'

He nodded, that smile ever more unnerving. 'You know about the revolution of the dead.'

'I do,' I said boldly, though the thought that such a

thing could be real made me want to run screaming. There was much I did not know, and of what I had been told by Celia and Luke, there was much I did not understand. Every hundred and fifty years, or seven generations, there is an 'agitation', an uprising of sorts. The last time was during the Civil War, when Luke was alive. Millions of living had perished, though balance between the living and the dead had ultimately been restored.

'And you are the Seventh,' Deus said. It was not a question.

'I am,' I replied.

I managed to say the words convincingly, though I wasn't quite sure what it meant. I knew the Lucasta women all had certain gifts. Madame Aurora, for instance, was a great fortune teller and the obsidian ring I wore had belonged to her. I was the Seventh Lucasta daughter, the one who came every hundred and fifty years at the time of the revolution, and my gifts were supposedly pretty specific to that. Somehow. Frankly the whole thing smacked a bit of those prophecies that I'd read about in my mother's books on ancient mythology and folklore – so many of which had not come to pass. I really, really hoped that would be the case with this whole revolution of the dead thing. Still, my great-aunt Celia put great weight on it. Luke seemed to as well.

'Lieutenant Luke told me that a powerful force was present in the house, and then he disappeared. Can you tell me why he disappeared, or what he meant?' I asked, trying again to get some information out of Deus.

'Myself, I do not see ghosts. It must be very strange for you,' he remarked.

Myself, I do not drink blood, I thought. *That must be strange also.*

I folded my arms. 'You are avoiding the question. Is this some sort of game for you?'

'Miss Pandora English, this is no game. I can assure you of that,' he said, leaning forward and gazing at me with an intensity that made the breath catch in my throat. 'The revolution of the dead is coming and when it does we will all be in peril. We will rely on you.'

'Rely on *me*? Because I am the Seventh?'

He nodded, still grinning, though I thought I detected something new in his eyes. Something sombre. A subtle hint of vulnerability even?

The idea of Deus relying on me, of all people, was frankly incomprehensible. He was the most powerful and self-assured creature I'd ever met. He was immortal, for heaven's sake. Or not *heaven's*, exactly ...

'So this powerful force you have come to warn me about is related to the revolution?'

'Perhaps.'

I sighed. 'But you believe this revolution is coming?' I said.

'It does not matter if we believe it. The revolution will come regardless.'

Okay. So Celia, Luke and Deus all really believed this prophecy. That much was clear. 'But why would you rely on me if the revolution came? You are – excuse me for saying so – undead.'

'No offence taken. I am not living.' He took another sip of his tea and put down his cup with a clink of china. 'And you are the Seventh. No one else can do what must be done.'

'What must be done ...'

'Yes, what must be done.'

I sighed again. Always riddles with Deus. He was as bad as Celia like that. They seemed unwilling or unable to give me straight answers. Yet even Luke had told me he was unable to tell me certain things, certain supernatural secrets.

In that moment I was tempted to press him about what that meant, yet Deus did not seem the right person to ask when Celia, as a Lucasta herself, would surely know more. Or perhaps I felt reluctant to ask Deus questions simply because I found myself eager to impress him? To seem like I was more confident than I really was. Was that his trickery at work?

'Perhaps you can explain this, then. Why, if you are not living, would the revolution be a problem for you?'

'You misunderstand my nature. I am not dead. I do not wish for the destruction of the living world. The undead require balance to survive. Without the living ...'

Without the living you would have no one to feed on.

We were both silent for a while.

'I need to know, is my boss, Skye DeVille, Sanguine now?' I found myself saying.

'We do not reveal our numbers,' was his immediate reply. It sounded rehearsed, I thought.

I took a deep, deliberate breath and folded my

arms again. 'Well, Celia told me about a bunch of different Sanguine. She named names, like Napoleon and Nietzsche and Marie Antoinette, and Frida Kahlo and Oscar Wilde, and even Queen Victoria, Widow of Windsor. Shall I go on?'

Deus chuckled softly. 'Some of those are rumours, and the others are well known,' he said, though I thought I detected a slight edge in his voice. I took it as irritation with the fact that Celia had given me names.

'I live among the living and I can tell you it is not well known that Queen Victoria is a va—' I covered my mouth. 'Um, that she is Sanguine,' I finished awkwardly.

I nearly said vampire *in front of Deus*. Of all the undead I could say the V word to!

'So surely you can tell me if Skye DeVille has been turned,' I said.

'Turned? Like a leaf?'

'Come on. She's my boss.'

'I am sorry. As I said, we do not reveal our numbers.'

'Unless they first reveal themselves?'

He nodded and then to my surprise, he stood.

'Now I must go, Pandora English, the Seventh.' He said the title with considerable respect. 'I regret that I cannot be more helpful.'

My throat constricted a little. I stood. 'Well, thank you for the ... warning.' Though it had not been much help at all.

Deus gave me a little bow, which I returned. It was an immense relief when he turned and left the room, walking back through the casket. The lid closed and

I stood in the antechamber for a while, holding my head.

We will rely on you.

＊＊＊

My great-aunt somehow looked more beautiful when I emerged. She'd redone her hair and makeup, those red lips perfectly painted, and she'd put on a striking lace dress that showed just the right hint of pale décolletage, accessorised with pearls and her usual black veil.

'Wow,' I said, taking in her transformation. 'You look lovely.'

'I have an appointment,' she said, grabbing her fox stole and wrapping it around her.

It looked more like a date than an appointment to me. Would she meet up with Deus?

'Are you okay? You seem a bit shaken,' she remarked.

I was shaken. That was true. Actually, I was downright exhausted, I realised. 'Deus came to warn me about some powerful new force in Spektor, though he couldn't say what it is. And well, you know, I thought for a second there that I was getting better at being around Deus, as you said I would. But ...'

My great-aunt bit her lip. *She actually bit her lip.* I hadn't seen this expression from her before.

'What? What is it?'

'About that ...'

My eyes widened. 'But you said I would be able to control it better, especially because I am the Seventh. You said that the Sanguine had that natural predatory ability, that mesmerising effect, but I would learn to become immune to it.'

'I did say that, and it is true, but not now, I'm afraid. It's because of his blood.'

'His blood?'

'You do remember, don't you? You drank his blood,' my great-aunt said patiently. She adjusted her stole.

'But it was only a sip, right? I wasn't even conscious!' I protested.

They'd made me drink it. When I had come to, I'd seen the wine glass sitting there, filled with red stuff, and it'd taken me a moment to register what it was. The idea of having drunk Deus's blood — anyone's blood — had been sickening to me. It still was. But Sanguine blood, particularly Deus's, was powerful and it had worked as an effective antivenene for the paralysing and potentially deadly spider bite I'd suffered. I'd probably have died without it.

I frowned. 'It was just a sip, wasn't it? Tell me it was just a sip.'

She tilted her head. 'A little more than a sip. It is very tasty.'

Ewww.

'That's why you're tanned. The blood makes you light sensitive.'

'No!' I screamed and grabbed my face.

She stepped towards me and placed a cool hand on my shoulder. 'Darling, there is no need for hysterics.'

'I have a tan because I'm becoming a vampire. Oh my God!' I started to shake.

'Language, Pandora. And anyway, you most certainly are not. Goodness, if everyone who sampled ichor happened to turn ... well, the balance of the undead and the living would become quite a problem indeed. Just use more sunblock for a while. It's best to stay out of the sun, anyway.'

I had thought my tan was strange for early spring in Manhattan. 'So I'm not turning?' I pressed.

'I should think not.'

I relaxed a touch. I had to believe she was right about this. I didn't want to end up like my Fledgling friend Samantha, nibbling on the wooden railings in the house like a teething puppy. Or worse, I didn't want to end up like Athanasia and her horrible friends.

I frowned. 'Wait. Ichor?'

I'd been raised on my mother's books on mythology, folklore and the beliefs of different cultures. Ichor was described as the ethereal nectar of the gods – their blood. I recalled the tale of Talos, a giant man made of bronze with huge wings, who had a vein of ichor running through his body, stopped with a nail in his back. As legend had it, when the sorceress Medea pulled out the nail, he bled to death. I hadn't heard the term used in relation to vampires.

'Wasn't ichor the word for the "nectar of the gods" in Ancient Greek mythology?' I asked.

'Indeed it was,' my great-aunt said and smiled slyly.

In ancient Crete they had believed in Talos. That was where the legend began, I realised. Perhaps that was why Celia used the term for Deus? He was a little godlike in certain ways and that was what his name meant in Latin. *Deus.* I thought of him again and shivered. I was so exhausted by our exchange in the antechamber. It had taken a lot to resist the temptation to just stare at him and succumb to his strange magnetism.

'So, will his blood, or ichor, or whatever it is, leave my body?'

'Eventually, yes. But in the meantime, Deus may have more of a hold on you than we'd hoped. Don't worry, you are strong and his hold will pass.' She patted me on the arm and left me, heading towards the antechamber. I felt sure she was going to see Deus, the ancient creature whose blood pumped in my veins. I watched her go, feeling exhausted and dispirited. It was late and I needed sleep.

And still, there was no sign of Lieutenant Luke.

CHAPTER
SIX

J stood barefoot on a grassy hilltop, dressed only in my long white nightgown, the one I wore each night. The hem of my gown rustled in the breeze, the light fabric pushing back against my body.

This hilltop was familiar to my dreams – a place of some nameless primal significance. I shut my eyes and tilted my face to the sun's comforting rays, letting the sunlight caress my eyelids, and I held my arms aloft, palms open. Next to me, silent and majestic, was a grand tree, roots snaking across the soil at my feet, its bare, twisted branches stretching up to the sky, reaching so much higher than I could. And above us both, all was bright and blue, with only the barest wisp of white cloud moving across the vast, clear, convex sky. In time I heard the tree breathe, and the sigh of the earth, her heart beating in time with mine, the sky above spinning slowly, ever so slowly.

For a while I held that sense of peace: that sense of somehow being part of the earth, part of that giant, magnificent tree, part of the ground I stood upon.

And then a visitor came.

There was a low rumble beneath me, the earth shaking, and I opened my eyes to observe a figure on horseback approaching. I knew immediately that it was Second Lieutenant Luke Thomas, astride his mighty white stallion. The steed's hooves pounded the earth and the vibrations shook my feet and caused the tree at my side to shrink back into its roots. Yet it was Luke, and so I welcomed him.

'Lieutenant Luke! I'm here!' I tried to call out, relieved to see him. But though I tried, I made no sound. The words died in my throat.

Smiling, my arms open, I watched him ride closer, a mere speck on the horizon at first, then growing steadily larger. He wore his dark blue uniform, his cavalry sword at his hip, the edges of his dark, fitted frockcoat catching the wind. His posture was formal and upright. The stallion he commanded began to neigh and whinny, and when he stopped before me, his horse bent down, kneeling, its magnificent head bowing. Lieutenant Luke removed his cap and inclined his head to me.

'Thank goodness, Luke,' I began but again my words would not come out.

Thunder cracked above us and immediately the bright sky turned a dark midnight blue, the pretty white clouds glowing an eerie green, morphing swiftly into something sinister, some alien force to be feared. They slithered through the air, terrifying and unnatural, coiling as if ready to strike. And that's when I saw the other figure – a figure in a black suit. I caught the movement out of the corner of my eye as the figure came towards us with unnatural speed, its legs unmoving as it rushed forward. Though all I could see was his silhouette, something about him gave me a terrible sense of foreboding. In seconds he was as close as Luke. So fast. He was already here.

I stepped back, fear taking me. The tree had been half swallowed up by the ground. Or perhaps it was trying to flee back to the earth.

'Luke, what's happening?' I tried to call out, but still I had no voice.

Luke lifted his head to look at me.

And I screamed.

I woke with a start on Friday morning. My bed sheets were in disarray, the lace-edged pillows strewn across the covers and on the floor. I sat up and scratched my head. Somehow, I felt Lieutenant Luke's proximity, as if we'd just been face to face, yet I had no idea whether or not I'd been visited by him.

Luke is gone.

He had not visited me, I recalled: he was still missing. Yet he'd been in my dream and something about him had been horrifying. What was it?

Hmmm.

I looked at the bedside clock. It was already past seven, I realised with a jolt. It was nearly time to leave for work. I needed to hustle.

'What happened? The date didn't go well?'

It was lunchtime when my friend Morticia approached me at my little cubicle, wide-eyed and eager to hear all about my mysterious date. 'What happened?' she asked again. 'You've looked miserable all morning.'

She'd noticed I'd arrived at the office five minutes late, which was unlike me. Pepper, the deputy editor, had noticed, too.

Oops.

Grinning one day, miserable the next. Perhaps it wasn't so good to have a dead boyfriend.

Yes, I was more than a bit glum and I shouldn't have been surprised that Morticia had noticed. I didn't know what to make of Lieutenant Luke's sudden disappearance, and since then I'd been feeling quite out of sorts. I looked around and saw that Morticia and I had a little privacy, giving us a moment to talk. (Pepper was out for lunch and Skye was just plain out. Or under the ground. It was impossible to know.) But what could I tell Morticia, really? I paused, considering my words, and in the end I merely shook my head.

'Oh, Pandora,' she said, and put a hand on my shoulder.

I shrugged. 'I'm okay. I'd just rather not talk about it right now.'

I didn't want sympathy so I thought I'd best shut it. My satchel was at my feet and I pulled it out and fished around for the bagel I'd packed. Morticia pulled a chair over from one of the empty desks and we sat side by side, eating our lunches.

'I'm really sorry it didn't go well,' she said between mouthfuls, genuinely trying to be helpful.

'It's fine. I'm going to cover this thing on Saturday night for our social page. Do you know anything about it?' I said, hitting on the perfect topic to change the subject.

Who needed to talk about boys, anyway? Boys from the Civil War, who made you feel like you were floating when you kissed ...

'Oh!' Morticia exclaimed suddenly, taking me by surprise. She sat up straight and put her sandwich down. 'So you did score an invite!' Her eyes were huge, more huge than usual. This thing was obviously a bigger deal than I'd realised. I hadn't given it a whole lot of thought, with everything else going on. 'I thought I heard her mention it to you but I was trying not to eavesdrop.'

I doubted Morticia had tried very hard not to hear.

'Well, I wouldn't call it an invite,' I said. 'I mean, Pepper just wants me to take photos.'

'That is *so cool*,' she declared, waving her hands around a little crazily. 'All the famous people will be there!'

'Really?' That seemed unlikely, technically speaking. Unless the venue was very large indeed.

'It's an annual thing,' she went on excitedly. 'I've always wanted to go.'

And I'd never even heard of it. *Maybe you can go and take the photos*, I nearly said, but I held my tongue. I was hardly in a position to reassign my duties.

I arrived home to Spektor after my day at *Pandora*, just as the final colours of a purple sunset faded to starry black. My boss Skye DeVille had not shown up all day (again) and, as promised, Pepper had given me her camera along with the address for the party on Saturday, plus a list of names of people to photograph and a media pass to get me in. The list included some pretty famous designers and actors, and the idea of meeting them, even just to photograph, gave me something to look forward to. It seemed possible that Morticia was right about it being an exciting event.

It wasn't quite enough to take my mind off Lieutenant Luke's MIA status, but it was something.

The walk through Central Park that evening was uneventful and the streets of Spektor looked as uninhabited as a ghost town as I passed Harold's Grocer and arrived at the front door of the mansion unmolested by my fanged neighbours. Yet when I put my key in the lock I immediately sensed that something was different. I couldn't say what it was or how I knew, but I was learning to trust my instincts, and my instincts told me something was up.

My stomach went cold.

Someone is here.

Or something?

Visibility was poor, the street particularly foggy. I looked both ways and pulled some rice from one pocket before I turned the key, unlocking the heavy door, worried some Sanguine supermodel might ambush me. The lobby was in absolute darkness, lights off. No sounds. No one lunging at me. Quickly, I flicked the switch and the big chandelier came on.

'Oh!' I cried and covered my mouth.

A woman hung from the chandelier.

She was dressed from head to toe in black, her long widow's veil cinched tight at the neck by a knotted rope, looped around the light fixture. Her black crepe veil was bunched up tightly across her face, showing the shape of a nose and the hollow of an open, screaming mouth. For one horrible instant I thought it might be my great-aunt Celia, as she was the only woman I'd ever seen wear a black veil. But the clothing was wrong. The figure hung from the chandelier in a dull, ankle-length black dress with long sleeves and a tight-laced bodice, the skirt made full with dark petticoats, giving her the shape of a funeral bell as she hung lifelessly, her small lace-up leather boots dangling. I recognised it as a turn-of-the-century mourning dress.

The woman spun slowly, the chandelier twisted to one side, and a thought flashed into my mind: *Has she always been there, twisting that chandelier?*

I needed to cut her down. Now.

The front door of the house slammed shut behind me and I jumped. When I looked again the woman was gone.

Impossible. She was right there.

'Um, hello?' I said to the empty lobby. The chandelier was askew, draped in cobwebs. 'Is anyone there?'

I was not afraid of ghosts, even faceless ones. Yet my heart was pounding quickly in my chest and my skin had come up in tiny bumps. The woman was gone but the strange feeling remained. What was it exactly? An energy? Or the opposite – something cold and deathly, like a new void in the house?

'Hello? Luke, are you here? Lieutenant Luke?'

There was no response.

CHAPTER
SEVEN

I knocked on the door and entered Celia's penthouse, shaken.

My great-aunt regarded me. 'Darling, you look like you've seen a ghost.'

I nodded, feeling jittery. 'I did.'

She tilted her head and narrowed her eyes. 'Well, I'm going to make us some tea,' she announced, and before I could protest she was sauntering towards the kitchen in her elegant slippers with Freyja trailing behind her.

Celia did make very nice tea, but I wasn't sure that could fix everything just now. Slowly, I placed my heavy satchel on the floor, took off my coat and hung it up, and slipped off my shoes, trying to absorb what I'd seen and, particularly, my reaction to it. The sight of that woman had really shaken me. It wasn't just that I'd seen a ghost because I'd been seeing ghosts for as long as I could remember. It was something else. Something about her. Or something about the new strangeness in the house that had seemed to arrive just as Luke had disappeared; just as he'd warned me.

That mouth. Open. With the black veil pulled tight across it.

Freyja came over to herd me gently into the kitchen, purring against my ankles and nudging me forward.

'How was work today?' my great-aunt asked casually over her shoulder as she put the kettle on, calmly absorbed in her ritual.

I leaned against the doorframe. 'Work was fine.' I paused. 'But there was a woman hanging from the chandelier in the lobby just now.'

She turned and cocked her head, the veil sitting against her high cheekbones. 'Well, then. Hanging from the chandelier?' she said, watching my face. 'And she is gone now?'

I nodded. 'But I did see her. She was there.'

'I have no doubt,' my great-aunt said. She prepared a tray with the lovely pot and cups, a little jug of milk and some cubes of sugar, and once the tea was ready she walked to the lounge room and sat down in her reading chair, the tray jingling a little. She placed the tray on the little table next to the chair and I perched myself on the edge of the leather hassock.

'The widow Elizabeth Barrett,' Celia said calmly, waiting for the tea to steep.

My eyes widened. 'Dr Edmund Barrett's widow? You think that was her I saw hanging from the chandelier?'

'Yes, the sad thing. She seems the most likely person. She'd been in deep mourning for a year before she hanged herself on the anniversary of her husband's death.'

Oh.

'Some people don't handle becoming widows very

well,' she said, and I thought of how well Celia had coped all these years. Being a widow hadn't exactly held her back; though, of course, I knew she had loved her husband very much. It must be incredibly hard to lose a partner like that. 'I believe she killed herself in the lobby,' she said.

Then it would have been from the chandelier, I thought. There was nowhere else to facilitate such a gruesome end.

The tea was ready, the pleasant and invigorating scent filling the room, as familiar as anything I'd come to know since moving here. Celia poured me a cup, and I added a sugar cube and a dash of milk and stirred, the little silver spoon clinking against the china.

'It sounds like Mrs Barrett, but I haven't seen her before,' I said and took a sip. I remembered Celia mentioning something of her, when she had first explained about the history of the old house. 'Great-Aunt Celia, the house feels different lately. Lieutenant Luke, before he vanished, said there was something powerful here. Um, you haven't seen Lieutenant Luke at all?'

'Your soldier? Well, no, not since you left together last night.'

Celia often called him that – my soldier.

'Though, of course, I don't normally see him. It is not my gift,' she added. Celia had gifts of her own, but communication with the dead was not one of them.

It had been a silly question. Of course, she would tell me if she'd seen him, which she couldn't unless he was flesh. I was grasping at straws.

'Deus said the same thing, something about a

powerful force.' I paused. 'Tonight I think I will explore the mansion,' I said, though the idea did frighten me somewhat, after seeing Mrs Barrett – if that's who the hanging woman was.

Celia nodded. 'I see.'

'Luke *has* to be here. I just can't accept that he's gone.'

'If you cannot accept it, perhaps you are right?' she replied. 'If that is what your instincts tell you.'

'Thank you for the cup of tea, Great-Aunt Celia,' I said when I'd finished. I excused myself and left the lounge room. Then I pulled the skeleton key from my satchel and held it firmly in my palm.

Right or wrong, I had to find out.

I took the lift, wrapped in my coat (with uncooked rice in the pockets), warily watching the dusty landings pass through the gaps in the dilapidated ironwork, a battery-operated torch in one hand and the skeleton key in the other. There was no movement and no noise save for the whine and rattle of the old lift. When I reached the lobby I stepped out and listened to the doors squeak shut behind me. Luke had to be somewhere. His spirit was trapped in this house. He couldn't just vanish.

'Lieutenant Luke? Are you here?' I said to the empty space in a voice that sounded uncertain to my own ears.

Usually, calling for him after dark was enough. But not now. Now there was no response except for the subtle creaking of the old house. I looked around me, frowning.

The cobweb-covered chandelier was on its standard angle, with no one hanging from it. I walked towards it and gazed up at the filthy crystals, wondering. Had it really been Elizabeth, as Celia suggested? Why would she appear now, about a century after passing on? Had she simply decided to reveal herself, or was it something else? Was it related to Luke's disappearance somehow?

In my periphery I saw something stir by the curving mezzanine stairs and in seconds I had slipped the key into my pocket in favour of some rice, the torch held in front of me like a club. My breath caught in my throat and I stood rigid, ready for anything.

A familiar figure rose on the stairs, standing up. 'Oh, Samantha! You gave me a fright,' I said, holding a palm full of rice to my chest.

'Hi Pandora,' she replied in her usual dejected tone and slunk towards me on bare feet, padding down the steps. Her blonde ringlets were dirty and her face appeared unwashed. She'd been sitting there so quietly I hadn't even noticed her.

'I haven't seen you around lately. Are you okay?' I asked.

She shrugged. 'Athanasia is away at the moment so I haven't had much to do.'

Samantha was a Fledgling, turned by Athanasia, and she now had a disturbing dedication to her every whim. Samantha was made to clean and polish the caskets of Athanasia's little gang, along with other chores. She was treated no better than a slave, and even though she'd tried to rip my throat out once, in a blind hunger, it pained me to see her treated that way. I felt sad for her family, too. They would have no idea what had happened to their daughter.

'They've not been saying very nice things about you,' Samantha told me in a small voice.

'Do you mean Blonde and Redhead?' *I'll bet they haven't been saying nice things*, I thought. 'Don't worry about that. Are they home at the moment?' I looked around to see if we had company.

She shook her head. So they were out. Probably hunting. The thought gave me a little shiver.

'Have they been treating you okay?' I asked, though I was pretty sure I knew the answer.

Samantha looked rather unwell, even for someone who was not quite alive. She was pale as parchment and almost as thin. I saw that she was still wearing the bland grey suit I'd given her. It hung on her bony frame like a rag. I'd bought it in Gretchenville, naively thinking it would make a good impression for my job interview at *Mia* magazine, which it certainly hadn't. Now the suit was frayed and spotted with dirt. I hadn't seen Samantha in anything else, and I knew for a fact that Blonde and Redhead hoarded excessive stacks of clothes in their room on the second floor. I'd tried to encourage Samantha to insist on being allowed to wear some of that clothing, but obviously that hadn't worked out.

'You know my friend Luke?' I said.

She shook her head, looking at her bare, dirty toes.

'But I've told you about him,' I reminded her. She'd never seen him but she had heard me talking to him. 'He died in the Civil War. He's a friend of mine. Remember I mentioned him?'

She nodded faintly, perhaps recalling our conversation. My next question was probably futile but I had to ask. 'Have you seen or heard anything about him? Maybe from the others?'

The Fledgling shook her head again. The movement was weak. It made me wonder if she was eating enough. Just what or who was she eating, anyway? I knew she'd taken to the rodents in the mansion, which was not a nice thought, though perhaps less morbid than the bloody alternative.

Samantha said nothing more, so it seemed time to say goodbye. 'Okay.' I reached into my pocket, letting the rice go and squeezing the skeleton key impatiently in my hand. 'Well, um, I'm looking for Lieutenant Luke, so if you hear anything I hope you'll tell me.'

She nodded.

Then I had a thought. 'Do you know of any hidden passageways in the house?' Her face remained blank. Sometimes it felt like I was talking to a rag doll – a limp, sad doll that was perfectly nice, yet dangerous when hungry. 'Any panels in the lobby that open up, that sort of thing?' I asked.

Yet all Samantha did was shrug again.

'Right. Do you know what's on the other side of the mezzanine door?' It was boarded up.

'Stairs,' she said in a voice so quiet I might have missed it.

I perked up. 'Did you say stairs?'

She nodded and a greasy curl fell over her eyes.

'Where do the stairs lead?'

'All through the house.'

'Can you get through the door?' I said and pointed up the staircase she'd appeared from.

'It's boarded up,' she said, cocking her head to one side, those cheekbones jutting out like knives. She seemed perplexed that I would not have noticed something so obvious.

'I know, but can you open it? Have you tried? Why is it boarded up?' I asked.

My questions were met with yet another limp shrug. She seemed to communicate almost entirely by shrug. 'The staircase doesn't get used, I guess. Because of the elevator,' she muttered.

It did make sense that there was a staircase that led to the lobby, though it seemed a little strange that it was boarded up at the bottom, whether the stairs were commonly used or not. That wasn't fire safe, to say the least, but then again, the mansion was unlikely to pass any safety inspection. Besides, most of the residents wouldn't have a problem with smoke inhalation, as they didn't breathe.

Creepy.

'Well, let me know if you hear about Luke or anything else that might be of interest, okay? And let me know if I can help with, um, anything,' I said awkwardly, reminding myself that she was Sanguine and I should therefore be cautious about committing myself too much.

Samantha nodded and slunk away again. *Alrighty*

then, I thought as I watched her go, her thin shoulders slumped. She cut a sad figure as she returned to her spot on the steps, evidently waiting for her master to return. She sure hadn't taken well to being turned.

I checked nearly every panel in the oval lobby, even the mezzanine door again, right behind Samantha, who sat eerily motionless and silent on the steps. I was about to give up when finally I felt a shift of air at the wall beneath the mezzanine stairs. Intrigued, I held my palms to the wall and noted a faint draught coming through. I flicked my torch on and shone it against the section of wall. *Yes.* There was a rectangular doorway, just tall enough for someone my height to walk through. It was hidden so cleverly by the low wooden panels that I'd looked at it before and failed to spot the slight edge. I ran my fingers over the wall, as if reading braille, and moved the torch beam across, searching.

And then I found it. A keyhole.

My heart quickening, I pulled the key from my pocket. *Yes.*

The skeleton key fit perfectly and I felt triumphant as the lock turned, the house finally revealing another secret to me, but though it was unlocked the door would not open. I leaned against it with my shoulder and pushed, but it wouldn't budge. *Come on.* I took a step back and then shoved against it with more force. It shifted only an inch.

Hmmm. 'Samantha?' I said, and her head appeared

over the edge of the steps. 'Can you please help me with this? If you're not, err, busy?'

She padded over to me, her expression vacant.

'There's a door here, but I need your help to open it,' I explained, and she shrugged her assent.

'Thanks,' I told her and put the torch down at my feet. 'Now, on the count of three, let's both push the door as hard as we can. Okay?'

Another shrug.

'One ...' I said, readying myself. 'Two ... three!'

We rammed our shoulders into the stubborn door, and though Samantha did not appear very strong she must have given it a good push, because the door flew open in a cloud of century-old dust.

I coughed, falling forward into the open doorway. 'Wow! Thank you. We did it!' I picked up the torch and shone it inside the dark entry, covering my mouth from the dust. It was a narrow corridor of some kind. Samantha didn't seem particularly interested in it − or anything else for that matter. I thanked her again as she walked away to sit on the mezzanine stairs.

Goodness. She really took the whole depressed vampire thing to a new level.

I pulled the key out of the lock, pocketed it, and stepped inside the cold, dark corridor.

Oh boy.

The space felt a bit damp, I thought, and like the chandelier it was draped with cobwebs. I sure hoped there weren't a lot of spiders around. I had developed something of an aversion to spiders recently. Holding my coat closed around me, I walked slowly, casting torchlight just beyond my feet to guide the way. The floor was laid with stones and it was a little uneven. Gradually it wound to the right, towards what I thought was the back of the house – though I quickly felt disoriented enough in the small space to be uncertain. The light from the lobby chandelier was long gone and only the torch lit the way. Occasionally the stone floor seemed to slope a little, and I came close to tripping several times. I had to watch my footing.

And that was why I didn't see her until I was practically at her toes.

Oh!

I looked up and before I could stop myself, I let out a short, sharp scream. It was the woman in black, faceless and silent, standing in the corridor with what looked like a candle in a silver candleholder, held in the frail fingers of her right hand. I stared into the featureless shroud and swallowed. The candle she held lit itself as I stared – *actually lit itself* – and in the low light, perhaps because of the dust in the corridor, the flame appeared green.

After what seemed like an eternity, my heart started beating again. 'Is your name Elizabeth? Um, Mrs Elizabeth Barrett?' I managed to ask the figure, my frightened voice barely audible. It was as if the air in the corridor snuffed out the sound.

Though her mouth – if she had one – did not move and she made no sound, I sensed an acknowledgement. Somehow, I knew. It *was* her – Dr Barrett's widow.

Elizabeth Barrett turned and walked down the corridor

away from me, that unnatural candlelight illuminating our path. She seemed to be leading me somewhere, and I found myself following and quickening my pace. Yet even when I dared to come up to her shoulder, squeezing close in the narrow corridor, I could not see her face beneath the layers of her widow's veil.

'Elizabeth?' I said again, but she did not respond.

We walked for a time along the twisting corridor, me trailing just beyond the hem of her long black mourning dress, her strange candle lighting the way. Time seemed to pause, or at least shift at an odd pace. Sometimes I felt sure I'd followed her for hours, and passed the same cobwebs, the same stretch of wall and stone.

'Where are you leading me?' I finally asked and she stopped abruptly, causing me to almost fall on top of her.

She turned sideways suddenly and vanished, through a door or wall, or perhaps simply into thin air, leaving me alone in the corridor deep within the bowels of the mansion. 'Mrs Barrett?' I cried, pounding my fist against the stone walls of the corridor. 'Where did you go? Where were you leading—'

An unnerving rumble cut my words short. I froze in place as the floor beneath me spoke.

Krrrrrraaaaiiiik.

My torch flickered. Was the battery . . . dying?

This can't be happening.

The torchlight flashed on and off, and then everything went dark.

'No!' I cried.

The corridor was completely black now. Had

Elizabeth gone through a door I could not see, or had she just disappeared? *You can always retrace your steps*, I thought, yet something within me doubted it and when I reached out, to my horror, there was nothing there. Nothing at all. My fingertips clawed at the damp air. How could I retrace my steps if the walls had gone? How had the walls suddenly vanished?

Don't panic. Don't.

But I did. I sure did.

'No, no, no ...' I began muttering, feeling the corridor close in on me in the darkness. I began to quiver, the useless torch shaking in my hand.

'Help!'

I felt something cold descend in the cramped corridor and a familiar white shape began to materialise out of the blackness in front of me. I held my breath for a moment, waiting. *Is that ...?*

And to my great relief, Lieutenant Luke appeared in uniform before me, the details of his features gradually taking shape. Still slightly opaque, he took off his dark blue cap and bowed his head to me.

'Miss Pandora,' he said by way of greeting, his eyes glowing blue. I slipped gladly into his embrace, his ghostly arms enveloping me.

'Thank goodness,' I muttered into the gold buttons of his frockcoat. 'I tried calling you so many times. I thought something terrible had happened to you. You left so abruptly. I can't tell you how relieved I am.' I held him tightly, savouring his embrace. 'I think I'm lost. And my torch won't work. And ... what is this place?'

'You are lost?' he said, sounding concerned.

My torch flickered on again in my hand, though I hadn't done anything to fix it. As it blazed, I looked at it, perplexed. And now that I could see again, the walls were there. The corridor was narrow, the floor uneven and sloped. Everything was just as it had been before Mrs Barrett disappeared, except now Luke was with me. 'Well, I thought I was lost.'

The house is playing tricks.

'You called me and I didn't come? I am sorry, Miss Pandora,' Lieutenant Luke said.

I looked into his sincere, bright eyes. In the torchlight I saw that his jaw was clenched, his brows turned up at the centre.

'I'm so glad you came back.'

'Please believe me. I would never leave you like that on purpose,' Luke said.

He was talking about our date. 'But what happened? You were with me in Central Park and then you just vanished.'

At my question he took a breath – or rather something that looked like one – and he shook his head. 'Miss Pandora, I do not know,' he replied. 'I was there in the park with you just now, and then I felt a pull towards the mansion, a very powerful pull. My body began to dissolve back into ghost form, and I ended up here, seeing you and feeling your distress.'

'But it's been a whole day,' I observed. 'It's Friday night now.'

'Is it?' he exclaimed, evidently shocked.

How odd, I thought. 'You don't recall anything at all?'

Luke replaced his cap, and it sat at an appealing angle, bringing to mind a star of the silver screen, caught in the spotlight of my unreliable torch. He appeared to think for a moment, then shook his head. 'No, I do not recall anything. It is peculiar, I agree. Though now I can see you have changed your dress,' he said, observing me. 'I thought I was with you only moments ago.'

'No. That was yesterday.' I frowned. 'Huh. Well, I'm very glad you're back. Maybe we shouldn't try getting you outside the mansion again for a while?' I gave him another appreciative squeeze. Even as a ghost he felt awfully good. 'I did push you into it. Maybe you weren't ready or ...'

'Miss Pandora, it is not your fault. You were only trying to help me to be free of my confines here.'

His confines. It did seem unbearably sad to imagine Lieutenant Luke being trapped in this mansion forever. How could that be right?

I looked around, shining the light up the corridor in both directions. 'What is this place? Do you know?'

'It appears to be one of the lower passageways,' he said. 'There are many hidden corridors here.'

'Before you disappeared you said there was a powerful force that you could feel in Spektor,' I reminded him. 'Tonight when I got home from work I found a woman dressed in mourning clothes in the mansion. I saw her hanging from the chandelier in the lobby and then she led me here but she disappeared and I became lost.'

Or the house made me feel like I was lost. 'Was it her that you felt before you disappeared? Does she have something to do with this?'

'I do not know, Miss Pandora.'

'Celia told me that she was likely the ghost of Mrs Elizabeth Barrett, Dr Barrett's widow. Does that ring a bell at all?' I asked.

'A bell? Did a bell ring?'

I was confused for a second. Ours was quite a generational gap at times. 'No, I mean, does she sound familiar to you?'

'Oh yes, Mrs Barrett is certainly familiar,' Luke explained. 'I remember them both from when they were alive. Mrs Barrett was a nice lady, though lonely even when Edmund was alive. He spent a lot of time in his laboratory, down here. She was greatly saddened by her husband's passing. And the circumstances were mysterious.'

Yes. Spontaneous combustion, supposedly. Celia had told me.

'It was a most unfortunate event,' he said.

Indeed. 'You know, I think she was trying to lead me somewhere and then something happened.' I had a thought. 'Do you know where Barrett's laboratory might be? It's down here somewhere, is that right?'

We had explored the mansion many times together, but I had never explicitly asked Luke to take me to it.

'I believe I do know, but I do not wish to get too near it. It is in the basement.'

The mere mention of it gave me tingles of anxiety and

excitement. I remembered Celia's warning, *Don't ever go beneath the basement.*

'But would you guide me there, if I asked?' There I was, pushing him again. I seemed unable to stop myself. 'I really want to see it,' I found myself saying. 'I have a feeling it is what Mrs Barrett wanted to show me.'

She had been trying to lead me somewhere, hadn't she? I couldn't help but think it had something to do with her sudden appearance in the mansion.

'And I'd really like to get out of this corridor,' I added. 'I think it tried to trick me.'

CHAPTER
EIGHT

This is it. After emerging from the strange, twisting corridor and going back up the lift, the way we were familiar with, Luke and I made our way through Celia's antechamber and down the stone staircase on the other side. We followed the stairway down several floors, and I noted an odd instinct to turn back (one I ignored), then Lieutenant Luke led me through a short, hidden corridor to a large wooden door.

'I believe it is here,' Lieutenant Luke said. He looked uneasy.

I was out of breath and frankly I didn't fancy my chances of finding the doorway on my own, yet I sensed that the corridor I'd been lost in earlier – the corridor I hadn't wanted to continue along – led precisely here. Perhaps it hadn't wanted me to find what was behind this door? Perhaps that was why I felt these conflicting urges to explore the basement or simply run off?

I fished the skeleton key from my pocket, Lieutenant Luke's presence comforting at my back. The lock in the door looked rusty. Biting my lip, I bent at the knees and carefully pushed the key inside. It took a moment of jiggling, but eventually the key slid all the way in. Luke and I exchanged looks. I took a breath and turned the key. The tumblers inside the lock shifted with a series of audible squeaks. I pushed on the heavy door with one shoulder, the movement bringing up a puff of dust. It made me pause to cough, though Luke, at least in his current form, seemed unbothered by it. On seeing that I would open the door, he immediately passed through it to check what was on the other side, and when I pushed the door fully open and stepped in, he was already standing stiffly next to a long metal table.

'Are you okay, Miss Pandora?' he asked. His eyes glowed blue in the dark space.

I nodded and covered my mouth. 'I don't think anyone has been down here for ... for decades at least,' I said through my fingers. 'Probably more like a century.'

So this is Barrett's laboratory. The one he spent so much time in, hidden away from his lonely wife ...

I held the torch in front of me and, squinting, took a step forward. A table held some rectangular object, covered in a dusty cloth. Another table held what looked like glass bottles – no, beakers. Luke was standing next to what appeared to be a large stainless steel tray in the centre of the room, though it was bare. Actually, it wasn't so stainless, I noted. Maybe they hadn't invented 'stainless steel' back when this thing was made.

Surely there had to be electricity down here? I groped around in the low light, swinging my torch from side to side.

There. A switch by the door.

I grabbed it and found it surprisingly hard to pull up the switch. After a bit of resistance it flicked into place. There was a loud, quick buzz, then all was silent for a second.

What the ...?

The space began to light up. Tubes and metal coils were strung between glass beakers, many of which now lit up like Christmas lights, flashing red and green. The room filled with a steady, rhythmic mechanical hum. It was rising up from the equipment. Some of the beakers had begun to steam. I jumped back as a large wheel next to me started to turn, cobwebs caught up in it like spinning yarn.

'Maybe I should shut that off.' I leapt for the switch. Who knew what the equipment was for or what it might do? I pulled the switch down, using all the strength in my arm, and in seconds the room went quiet and dark.

I breathed a sigh of relief.

'I think I've found the light switch,' Luke said.

My torch was still lit (thank goodness) and I walked over to him and flicked on the switch he'd found. A huge circular light came on over the steel table in the middle of the room.

'Is that a surgery table ... or ...?'

Weird.

The whole place was weird. There were stacks of books and papers strewn about, and glass containers of all kinds. Everything was coated in a thick layer of dust and the liquid in most of the beakers had dried up on the bottom, though some of them still had just enough left to let off some bubbling steam. Jars were filled with dark liquid, like formaldehyde. I noticed a whole green frog floating in one, lifeless and alien looking. One item in particular gave me shivers – a large metal chair, fitted with thick leather straps and buckles. Spikes on the chair seemed connected to cables and electrodes of some kind. I shuddered to think what it was used for.

'Dr Edmund Barrett's laboratory. I've heard so much about it. I didn't know what to expect,' I said.

According to Celia, Barrett had hidden this space away from his wife. She hadn't known the nature of some of his experiments, or perhaps she had known and disapproved of them or was distressed by what he was doing. In any event, it seemed he'd sealed his laboratory away where it was hard to find.

'Look,' Luke said.

At one end of the room was a doorway, set ajar. I joined Luke and peered into a small study, charred black on two of the four walls, from where a fire of some kind had whipped through. Or perhaps not whipped through, exactly. Was this where Barrett had died, supposedly of spontaneous combustion?

'I think this is where Dr Barrett passed into the other world,' Lieutenant Luke said, echoing my thoughts.

I nodded. 'It certainly appears so.'

Celia told me his journals had been destroyed in the fire, along with all of Dr Barrett – except his feet and shoes. When they'd found him there had been nothing else but ashes left, apparently.

Books were scattered about the study in haphazardly stacked piles. I wondered if someone had tried to tidy the space after the fire, or if Barrett had simply stored his books that way. One interesting book sat on the edge of the lightly charred desk, though it was in reasonably good condition. *Transcendental Magic, its doctrine and ritual* by Eliphas Levi, it said. The title intrigued me. I picked it up and tucked it under my arm, thinking it might make an interesting addition to Celia's library.

'Miss Pandora, can we leave now?'

I looked at Luke and saw his concerned expression. 'What is it?'

'I do not wish to seem a coward, but I do not like this place. I feel that I should not be here.'

I felt it, too. The urge to leave. Yet my desire to learn more about Barrett and the house outweighed the instinct to flee. 'Is it not safe?' I asked.

'For me, I fear it is not.'

Lieutenant Luke had not wanted to seek this place out at all, I reminded myself. Now that I knew where it was and that the skeleton key fitted the lock, I could return at another time without him. (If I could find it again.)

'We can go if you like.'

He nodded and I wondered again what he was afraid of.

Luke followed me out through the laboratory. I turned the light off as we went, and locked the door after us. How intriguing to think that the man who had designed this strange and extraordinary house had spent so long locked away in that space, and yet no one had wanted to – or dared to – make use of all that equipment and all those books since.

'Enough exploring for now. Come with me,' I said and took Luke's ghostly hand, which felt cool and misty in mine.

I wanted to bring him up to my room so we could sit and chat as we used to, and perhaps even figure out what had gone wrong when we'd embarked on that ill-fated date of ours. I led Luke back up the staircase that snaked through this end of the house, the stone passages lit with heavy, wrought-iron torches, the flames throwing shadows against the old stone walls. 'It's so interesting that Barrett built all these secret passages, don't you think? It's like the residential part of the house is totally separate,' I remarked as we climbed through the passages that connected the two halves of the house. 'Barrett probably didn't want guests to stumble across what he was doing. Can you imagine? I mean, what or who did he strap into that chair? Or perhaps you saw all that in your time here?'

Luke was silent. I stopped and turned. 'Are you okay?' I asked him, still holding his hand.

Lieutenant Luke nodded in reply, but the gentle vulnerability in his eyes was too much to resist. I instinctively embraced him, tucking the book and torch into his lower back, my position on the stairs making us a similar height for once. 'I'm sorry. Thanks for leading me to the laboratory,' I said. 'I've been really curious about it.' I pulled back to look at him and in the low light of the torches in the stairwell, his beauty was otherworldly, illuminated as if by romantic candlelight. He still had that sense of tension about him. It had not faded entirely after we had left the lab.

'Why did you want to leave so urgently?' I asked.

He looked conflicted and uncertain.

'Maybe if you feel there is some ... energy there, it's because it's in the basement?' I postulated. 'Celia told me never to travel below the basement. I promised her I wouldn't.'

'Your great-aunt is wise,' he told me gravely.

She hadn't told me why. I had to admit, I was curious.

'Miss Pandora, promise me too that you won't go down there below the basement.'

'Why? What is it?'

'I cannot say,' Luke told me.

How frustrating, I thought. 'Is this one of those supernatural rules?'

'There are some things I am not permitted to say.'

But you are my spirit guide, I thought. It was no time for a fight though, especially so soon after his return, so I held my tongue.

'I'm just so glad you came back. I was really worried about you,' I told him, and put my arms around him again. He fitted his strong arms around my waist and hips and I lay my head on his shoulder for a moment. Now that I was holding him tight, I didn't want to let go. And the lab and all the things about this strange house that intrigued me so much seemed not to matter.

I closed my eyes and tilted my head to one side, and we kissed right there on the steps. With his cool kiss

I felt that wonderful lift he gave me, that rising up inside, which was quite apart from the height advantage of the stair I was on, quite apart from the purely physical. With Lieutenant Luke's strong hands caressing my waist and his soft mouth on mine, I felt I was floating, I felt I was somewhere else entirely – not in a tight stone stairwell in an old house full of wonders and dark secrets.

Our lips parted and I had no time to enjoy the usual afterglow of our shared caress. I pulled back suddenly, coming back down to earth in an instant.

His ghostly form had stiffened strangely. 'Luke? Are you okay?' I asked, opening my eyes.

He brought both his hands to his cap and appeared to squeeze his head.

'What is it?'

Luke took a step backwards, nearly tripping on the stairs. 'No ...'

He took another step back, and opened his eyes.

His eyes glowed *green*.

'Your eyes, Luke! What's happening?'

His stare was cold, terrifying and alien, and before I had the chance to say another word, he lunged forward, grabbing for my throat with both hands. I threw myself back onto the steps, evading his fingers, scrambled to my feet and ran up the stairs with a speed I did not think I was capable of. Something was seriously wrong with him.

I did not slow down until I was pushing up the lid of the casket, desperate for the safety of Celia's penthouse.

Bending at the knees, I closed the lid, careful not to let it slam, and then I sat on it, listening keenly while tears streamed down my cheeks. My great-aunt's antechamber was dark, except for the flickering candles. All was quiet below me. Lieutenant Luke had not followed. If he had, he might have been able to pass right through the floor if he wanted to, which was a terrifying thought.

Why had he tried to grab my throat? What was wrong with his eyes?

I closed my eyes tight and tried to calm myself, clutching the old book like a lifeline.

After a few minutes I finally stood up, and with a heavy heart left the hidden portal and made my way to the stone steps leading towards the penthouse. I glanced back at the casket one last time, and on seeing that the lid was safely in place, I opened the door and stepped into the hallway of the penthouse. I locked the door behind me using the skeleton key, hoping that would hold back any unwanted visitors. (Would it?)

I let out an audible exhalation.

Oh, hell, Luke ...

'Pandora, darling, are you all right?' Celia asked.

Feeling heavy, I left the torch by the door and walked to the lounge room, carrying the dusty book I'd found in the strange laboratory. Under the light of her reading lamp and the glow of a moon which still looked close to full, my great-aunt was perched elegantly in her reading chair again. She had been studying an old tome with Freyja curled up next to her and now she looked up and examined my expression. Though Celia could not be found earlier, when Luke and I had walked through, now she seemed not to have moved, yet my life had shifted profoundly.

'Okay ... I'm really worried now,' I said, for lack of a more articulate response to what had just happened.

He reached for my throat!

'Would you like a cup of tea?' Celia said, marking her page.

'Oh.' I screwed up my face and rubbed my forehead with one hand. 'That is very kind but I just don't think I can have another cup. I think I'm kind of freaking out, actually.'

My great-aunt raised one arched eyebrow and crossed her arms. I guess she didn't like the rejection a whole lot.

'I'm sorry. It's just that ... well, I found Lieutenant Luke, finally, and what I think was Dr Edmund Barrett's laboratory. But Luke is not Luke. Or Luke was Luke for a moment, but then ...' I rambled, making little sense. 'Oh, Great-Aunt Celia, I'm so worried. I found him, but he's not himself,' I said, and slumped back against the wall. My eyes started to well up again but I tried to calm myself. I was not going to cry anymore. I was not.

I heard Celia stand up and walk across the hardwood floor. Freyja darted over to me to sit at my feet, gazing at me with her big, strange opal eyes. I could swear she wanted to tell me something.

'He's just ... just like a zombie or something,' I muttered through my fingers, disbelieving. 'He's like someone else entirely. He looked at me like he didn't even know me, and then he tried to attack me.'

Had *I* done this? By making him leave the house? Had I asked for too much? Had I cursed him?

'And his eyes! His eyes glowed this horrible green.'

Celia put a cool hand on my shoulder. 'It sounds like someone or something has possessed your soldier friend,' she said calmly.

I blinked back the tears that had threatened to return and crossed my arms over my chest. Was that what had happened? 'What kind of something?' I asked.

I could tell by the look on her face that she had an idea.

'Let's have some tea,' she replied and turned on her elegant heel. I had to restrain myself from screaming. I desperately wanted to know what she meant, but I knew better than to push Celia. Celia did not allow herself to be hurried by anyone.

She's not going to let me refuse, is she? 'Okay,' I said, resigned to yet more tea.

My wise great-aunt walked into the kitchen, the beautiful fabric of her dress swishing as she moved, and I followed her without another word, feeling more than a little frustrated by this ritual of hers. She put the kettle on and I dutifully opened the cupboard and got out the cups and saucers. We went about our preparations silently, with Freyja pacing at our heels, clearly as impatient as I was. But before long we had the silver tray prepared and the penthouse smelled of aromatic tea leaves. We sat in the lounge room – Celia in her usual reading chair, and me perched on the hassock with Freyja purring in my lap.

'You have been through a lot this evening,' Celia said

as she carefully poured me a cup of tea and added a generous amount of milk and honey.

She handed me the cup and I thanked her. It smelled truly wonderful, and though I'd thought I was too stressed out to be able to relax, the first sip made my shoulders drop. The tea tasted sweet and milky compared to the last cup, only a couple of hours earlier, when I'd been upset by the woman hanging from the chandelier. But now seeing the woman in black seemed like nothing.

Luke. Not Luke . . .

I took another sip of the tea and felt my shoulders drop another inch. My great-aunt watched me carefully, I noticed, perhaps deciding whether her calming tea was taking effect.

It was.

'So you found your soldier but he was not himself?'

I shivered thinking about those eyes – those green eyes. 'Not at all,' I said.

'Well, you are safe now and that is the main thing. I'm sure there is an explanation.' She took a sip of her tea, her movements languid. 'What is that book you brought with you?' she asked casually.

'Oh yes.' I'd put it at my feet. 'I thought you might find this interesting. It's called *Transcendental Magic, its doctrine and ritual.*' I bent and picked it up, shaking the dust off the cover.

'Magus Eliphas Levi – the pen name of Alphonse Louis Constant, the French occultist. Alphonse did know some things,' Celia conceded. 'Though many of his ideas were quite fanciful. He believed that "souls" were sent out in pairs from heaven, and that when a man renounced the love of women, he made the bride who was destined for him a slave of the demons of debauch. No word on what happened to a man when a woman didn't care for him. There is a lot of that sort of nonsense in there.' She took another sip of tea. 'But on certain rituals, Alphonse was quite learned. Anyway, it should make for some interesting reading, though the various translations can be inexact.'

Celia seemed quite familiar with the tome. I opened it at the copyright page and noted that Barrett's edition had been published in 1896, a few years before his death. 'This translation is by a G. Redway.' I put the book in my lap and crossed my arms. 'I've been wondering about something. If Barrett's laboratory is so hidden, who discovered his body? How did they know he'd even died?'

'Dr Barrett had research assistants from time to time. Some of his experiments required it.'

'What happened to them?'

'Well ...' She paused. 'Let's just say no one saw much of them while they worked for Barrett, or after. I heard that Barrett's assistant at the time of his death was mute.'

Convenient if you didn't want them blabbing about your experiments, I thought. And not everyone in Edwardian days was literate.

'In any event, after Barrett's death, his assistant disappeared into a life of anonymity. Hopefully a happy one, but with Barrett's reputation, perhaps it was not good to let it be known you'd worked with him.'

Indeed.

'What does the book say?' Celia asked me, turning my attention back to its pages.

I shrugged. 'Well, it doesn't look like light reading. The writing style is quite antiquated.' I casually flipped through the book, stopping at a random page. It read:

We must collect in the first place, carefully the memorials of him (or her) whom we desire to behold, the articles he used, and on which his impression remains.

'Hmmm. This section is on necromancy, and it mentions needing to have articles of the deceased.'

'Does it?' she said, and her tone implied that it was not a question at all.

The sword. Barrett had had Luke's sword. I was more certain than ever that Barrett had tried to evoke him, though for what reason I could not fathom.

'But if all this is related somehow – Luke's disappearance, his sudden change – who is causing it? He hasn't been like this before.'

Celia took a slow sip of her tea and placed her cup and saucer back on the tray with a barely audible clink of china. 'There are two main forms of necromancy, Pandora.'

'Necromancy? You think Luke is being controlled by necromancy?' I blurted in response.

She nodded.

Of course he is. He is dead.

'The first form of necromancy involves a journey to the realm of the dead to consult with those who have departed from this world,' she explained.

'The realm of the dead? You mean, like, the Underworld?' I asked.

Luke had explained to me that there is an Underworld of some kind, but not hell, per se. Or at least not hell as it has been taught in religious scriptures over the centuries, with fire and brimstone and all that. What would such a place be like? Could the Underworld really *be* a physical place? A place a necromancer could travel to? Or was it a place you travelled to in your mind?

'Like the Underworld, yes,' Celia confirmed, continuing with her explanation. 'The second form of necromancy involves summoning spirits into the mortal sphere.'

Spirits like Luke, I thought.

'Both of these forms of necromancy aim to consult with or control spirits, and glean power or information from them, as spirits are known to possess great truths the living cannot know. The methods of summoning the dead or consulting with them differ, but there have been many famed necromancers over the centuries and a number of them left very specific instructions as to what methods may be used.'

I thought about that. Dr Edmund Barrett had clearly been dabbling in necromancy, and the discovery of Luke's cavalry sword in the mansion further lent credibility to the idea that Luke's grave had been disturbed by him, or someone working for him. I swallowed and tried to put the idea of Luke's decomposed remains out of my mind. I simply couldn't think of him like that, even after the way he'd been tonight, the way he'd changed.

'You said that spirits are known to possess truths the living cannot know. What kind of truths?' I asked.

I had already learned about a number of eye-opening supernatural rules since moving to Spektor. For instance, I could not contact Luke during the day. This despite the fact that I sometimes saw other supernatural creatures during the day, like the spider goddess, when she was at the height of her powers. Also, the Sanguine who inhabited the house could not enter a place where they had not been invited, hence Celia's penthouse was off limits. But this particular supernatural rule about forbidden truths caught my interest because it made me think of something Lieutenant Luke had told me. He had tried to explain that there were things he simply could not express, because he was forbidden from doing so, just as he was unable to venture outside the mansion in spirit form. These were the rules and not only was he obliged to uphold them, but he was also physically (spiritually?) unable to break them, even if he wished to.

All these rules were very mysterious to me.

'Truths,' my great-aunt said, typically vague, and gave me a significant look.

Right. So she's not going to explain that one, I thought. Or, she really doesn't know.

'Historically, necromancers used their skills for divination, fortune telling and so on.'

I nodded. I remembered some of what my mother's many textbooks on ancient cultures and beliefs had taught me about the practice. The word came from the Greek 'nekos' and 'manteia' – *dead divination.*

'There are thought to be many places which are ideal for the practising of necromancy – subterranean vaults and tombs, the ruins of ancient castles or monasteries, certain woods and deserts, certain crossroads – always at night and especially around the hour of midnight. But the most powerful necromancer or sorcerer can operate nearly anywhere and anytime.'

'There are sorcerers?' I asked, wide-eyed.

'There are many things in this world and the next,' she said.

Oh boy.

'You are a kind of necromancer, Pandora.'

'I'm a what?'

'You can summon the dead. You can speak to them. Surely you have thought of this before?'

I had always been able to speak with the dead, but they had come to me, not the other way around. It had made my childhood very difficult. I hadn't meant to do it – on the contrary. And I certainly hadn't set about finding an ancient castle or subterranean vault! Yes, I had been summoning Luke, but I'd been doing it without even thinking. Well, he'd *asked* me to summon him. He'd started coming to me whenever I'd needed help. Was that necromancy?

'But they come to me,' I protested.

'Pandora, listen to me. You have the powers of a necromancer. That is not something to be ashamed of. It is a special gift – an important gift for you, as long as you use it for good.'

I frowned. 'What do you mean?'

Celia picked up her cup of tea and gazed at the dark liquid, and through the black mesh of her delicate widow's veil I thought I detected concern etched on her smooth features. 'Necromancy can be dangerous,' she said gravely. 'If you use those powers by force, as many have over the centuries, it can be very dangerous indeed. There was a famous Egyptian necromancer named Chiancungi,' she explained. 'Seventeenth century, I believe. A famed fortune teller. According to legend, he perished while attempting to summon the spirit of Bokim.'

'The spirit of ...?' Growing up, I had read a lot of stories and folklore, but I had not heard of Chiancungi or Bokim.

'According to the tale, a so-called demon or infernal spirit by that name was summoned,' she said.

'A so-called demon? Demons exist? Why would anyone want to summon a demon?'

Necromancers? Sorcerers? Demons? I had to try to slow down and stop interrupting Celia, though my head was spinning.

The corners of Celia's perfectly painted red lips turned up just a touch. 'Always the questions with you,' she said, but there was a hint of pride in her voice. 'Demons are not as you may understand them.' She patted my hand with her cool fingers, and Freyja stretched her neck up to rub her face against her wrist. 'There are many misunderstandings about their kind – even more misunderstandings than there are about the Sanguine. Demons – or Dark Beings as they are more properly known – come in many forms, and they are very powerful, and possess much knowledge. Chiancungi did indeed try to summon Bokim. As the story goes, it was for a bet.'

I tried to imagine betting on whether or not I could raise a demon. I couldn't.

'Bokim was a particularly powerful Dark Being. Chiancungi waited until the ideal hour and he performed all of his usual ceremonies, in a deep cave chosen for its supernatural power. He draped the cave in black and made the traditional safe circle for himself and his assistant, who happened to be his sister, Napula. But after several hours of the ceremony, when Bokim did not manifest, he grew tired and impatient. Eventually they stepped outside the safety of the sacred circle, not realising that the spirit of Bokim had been summoned but could not yet be seen by human eyes.'

My eyes widened.

'Bokim seized them and crushed them to death.'

I swallowed.

'To answer your other question, the summoning of demons and other spirits is usually done to gain knowledge, or in an attempt to gain some kind of other power, though Chiancungi was particularly foolish to use it for a bet. Necromancy of this kind is a form of slavery, and when spirits are forced into submission, made manifest against their will and required to speak and give up their secrets, it makes them resentful and angry.'

I could understand that.

'It is unwise to use such a power unless it is absolutely necessary.'

I nodded. 'You told me Dr Barrett was thought to have been dabbling in necromancy before his death?'

'It was rumoured, yes.'

'Could this be ... related somehow?' I asked.

'Undoubtedly,' my great-aunt said. 'Undoubtedly.'

Then she leaned forward and caught my eye with as intense and striking a gaze as I had ever seen from her.

'There is someone here, Pandora. Beware this necromancer.'

I swallowed.

'Who? Who is here?'

'I'm afraid time will tell. And probably soon,' she said, not very reassuringly. 'Now, you look exhausted, darling,' she said, sitting back. 'You've had a big day and you should get some rest. Tomorrow is also a big day for you. You should try to sleep in. You need to rest while you can.'

I wasn't sure what she meant but it sounded a bit ominous.

'The party is tomorrow,' she reminded me.

I felt the sweet, milky tea working through my muscles and nerves, calming me. 'Of course,' I said. It was the weekend now. I could finally catch up on my sleep. 'Well, I suppose I should get to bed.'

Though I wondered how I would sleep when the image of Lieutenant Luke's glowing green eyes still burned in my mind.

CHAPTER
NINE

When I woke on Saturday I was sure I'd suffered terrible nightmares. I rose from my bed, feeling the dead clinging to me. I washed my face with cold water and stared down at my reflection, seeing fear and worry in my amber eyes.

Luke, what has happened to you?

Celia had once explained that dreams can be very revealing, and that some dreams can even act as important premonitions, but if that were true of these nightmares, I did not want to know what the future held.

It felt far too bleak.

It took me until late afternoon to finally get my courage up. I wasn't going to tiptoe around Spektor like a coward. I was the Seventh. I had to try to fix whatever had happened to Luke and find out what was going on in my new hometown. (If town was the right word.)

With plenty of time before I had to get ready for the party, I entered the locked antechamber in the penthouse. The sun had not yet gone down, so it was as safe a time as any. Still, I walked in carrying the battery-operated torch and Luke's sword, ready for anything. I would return to the discovery I'd made with my possessed friend the night before. I felt it had to offer more clues.

Hopefully those clues would not involve Luke lunging at me again.

The antechamber was dark and I heard no movement as I entered. The candles were not lit, though the faint scent of incense lingered. Celia did not seem to be up yet.

It felt strange to kneel on the floor and *voluntarily* open a coffin. Nothing good can generally come from opening a coffin. But this one was different, of course. I lifted the lid and shone the torchlight down the stone steps and I realised that I couldn't be sure if the Sanguine were unable to wake during the day, in the shelter of these cold, windowless corridors. I would put nothing past them. Or this house. I had the sword at least, and I wasn't afraid to use it.

I needed all the protection I could get.

Breathing slowly and evenly, I climbed down the narrow steps and into the stone passageway, my torch in one hand and the heavy sword in the other. Above me, the twisting stairwell led up to the roof of the mansion. But below – that was where I needed to go. Again, the old wrought-iron torches were lit in the cold stairwell, the open flames dancing orange and crimson. They seemed to always be burning, and, oddly, there was a faint smell of sulphur that became stronger the deeper I descended. I took the steps slowly, listening for movement and holding the sword in front of me, the sharp tip ready. Negotiating that cleverly hidden corridor, which only became visible in the low light when I stood at the right angle, I finally arrived in the basement. On the threshold of Barrett's fascinating abandoned laboratory, I pulled out the skeleton key.

Then I hesitated.

No.

I looked at the wooden door and then at the old key in my hand and felt a strong urge to turn back. Every fibre of my being was possessed with dread. *Go. Leave here, Pandora.* It was like the feeling I'd had in the corridor when my torch had gone out, everything telling me to turn back. I found myself pocketing the key, barely in control of my choice to do so. I did not even try the handle of the door.

My enthusiasm for exploration seemed, for the moment, to be utterly snuffed out, and a formidable fear and self-doubt had taken its place. I grabbed the sword and torch and climbed the stairs back to the safety of Celia's penthouse, feeling like a coward.

I took my time getting ready for the society party I had to cover for *Pandora*. When I was anxious I tended to take too long to decide what to wear, yet I knew that on this occasion it was more than that. I was aware of doing something normal, something people did every day.

This was a distraction.

When I was finally ready I stepped out into the lounge room, where Great-Aunt Celia and Freyja were waiting.

'What do you think?' I asked and did a little spin.

For tonight's work event I'd chosen a black and white vintage 1940s dress, with a crossover shape at the bust and a fitted waist, the silky, pleated fabric falling elegantly to the knee. It billowed out a bit when I did my spin. I was wearing the dress with the pair of vintage Mary Jane heels Celia had given me. They were ruby red, with a cute little strap across the instep. They seemed almost magical with all the adventures I'd imagined they'd seen. I'd worn them on my first date with Jay, I now recalled – the one where everything seemed to be going so well, before it became all too clear I could never have a boyfriend like normal girls did.

And now my beautiful but not so normal date had turned into a literal green-eyed monster. I just couldn't win.

'Don't worry,' Celia assured me, reading my mind, or at least my expression.

True, I did feel a bit anxious, and not only about the situation with Lieutenant Luke. Swish social gatherings for celebrities and fashion types were not my natural habitat, to say the least. I'd not even been to a lot of parties in Gretchenville, let alone anything like a society party on Park Avenue.

My great-aunt stood with one hand on her hip, giving me the kind of appraisal one might expect from a designer, her eyes moving over each detail of the outfit with a kind of quick, technical precision. 'You look wonderful,' she finally announced to my relief. 'It suits you very well. What is the dress code for the party?'

Pepper hadn't mentioned a dress code, I now realised.

'Cocktail, I think. Thank you for lending me this, Great-Aunt Celia. It's a really pretty dress,' I said, complimenting her design. I adjusted the tailored sleeves, which had small pleats and closed with neat double buttons just above the elbows. 'It was probably for some really glamorous movie star. Do you think it's all right on me?' I asked, though I was really thinking, *Am I pretty enough for it?*

'Pretty? Who needs pretty?' Celia shot back. 'Pretty can be fun, but it is optional, darling. If it fits and you feel good in it, that is the real currency. And you look stylish, which is much more timeless and interesting than mere prettiness. The people you work for value style. Was Diana Vreeland pretty? Was Coco Chanel pretty?'

She was right.

'They were smart and driven women. They were certainly stylish, but pretty? No.' She looked me over. 'You do happen to be pretty whether or not you know it, but the point is, you don't have to be. It's not about that. Though I do think this outfit could benefit from a touch of red to match the shoes.'

'Oh, yes, of course,' I said, straightening up. I had forgotten to put on any lipstick.

My great-aunt walked off towards her end of the penthouse and I found myself in the lounge room alone.

Okay.

I wanted to look right for the event, so maybe I should do as Celia suggested? It's true I still wasn't very good at blending in with the fashion crowd. On the dresser in my room I had a bit of makeup, so I went back and fished around for a red lipstick. I put it on carefully. I did not have the deft hand for it that my great-aunt did. She seemed to be able to apply her own makeup without even looking. Once I'd blotted my lips with a tissue I had a look. It did seem to work with the 1940s dress. Back then women seemed never to leave the house without ruby lips. I guess Celia was right. It was an evening event, after all.

I stepped out of my room and closed the door. Celia was back in the lounge room and she had a midnight-blue velvet box in her hands.

'I've got something for you to borrow,' she said and unclipped the little lock on the jewellery box. She opened it and I found myself staring at a stunning pendant on a thin white gold chain.

'Is that ... a ruby?' The stone was square cut, with a little diamond set on the edge of each corner, surrounded by a thin and delicate swirling motif.

My great-aunt nodded. 'I bought this for myself after winning my first big contract to design the costumes for a Rita Hayworth movie.'

'Rita Hayworth? Wow. Oh, Celia, it is so special. You can't let me borrow this.'

'But I must. It will look wonderful on you. And there's no use letting it sit in a drawer.' She pushed it towards me. 'Go on.'

I reached into the box and picked up the necklace by the chain, admiring the way the ruby shone as the light hit it.

'I'll help you,' my great-aunt said. She took it from

me and did up the clasp behind my neck while I held my hair up. When I let my hair down, the pendant fell into position just above the decolletage.

'Perfect.'

'Are you sure? This must be very valuable.'

'I'm sure,' she said, and put a cool, reassuring hand on my shoulder. 'It suits you.'

I nodded and held the stone against my chest. 'Thank you. I promise I will take good care of it.'

'I hope that you have a wonderful time,' she said. 'Vlad is waiting, when you are ready.'

Naturally, she had insisted that I use her chauffeur and, as it was pretty impossible to get taxis in Spektor because the place simply didn't exist on maps, it didn't seem the time to refuse her offer. I certainly had no intention of walking to Park Avenue in these shoes.

'Thanks, Great-Aunt Celia,' I said, and waved goodbye with a lump in my throat.

It didn't take too long to get to Park Avenue, with Vlad at the wheel. As we neared the address Pepper had given me, I spotted a red carpet ahead and the strobes of camera flashes lighting up the night. So the event was already in full swing. Good thing I'd arrived when I did. If I'd missed any of the important guests I'd be in trouble. Pepper had given me the names of guests she wanted photographed but very few other details. Interestingly it appeared to be a house party. For some reason that surprised me.

The car stopped at the kerb just beyond the red carpet and Vlad opened his door.

'No! Please don't,' I protested, but he was already out and coming around to my side to open the back door. As soon as it opened the sounds of the party spilled into the car – live music and the din of chatter and clinking glasses. I readied myself and stepped out onto the footpath to see a uniformed valet. Perhaps he'd intended to open the door for me, but instead he stood rigidly regarding Vlad with what looked like thinly veiled fear. He said nothing. Vlad closed the door and stood stoically next to Celia's car, expressionless in his dark sunglasses, while I made my way to the steps leading up into the house.

Oops.

I had wanted to make a subtle entrance without anyone noticing the strangeness of my driver, but never mind. At least no one had taken any photos. Vlad would be waiting for me when I needed to leave. I didn't have a number to call him but somehow I gathered that wouldn't matter. He seemed to spend his time waiting. He was nothing if not dedicated to Celia's commands.

The mansion was four storeys tall and took up one corner on Park Avenue. It was quite unlike any home I had been invited to. Surely it had to be the biggest freestanding house in Manhattan, not counting Celia's mansion in Spektor? Celia's place was strangely beautiful in its way, of course, but though this early 1900s home had been built in a similar era it was something else entirely. Far from being cobwebbed and aged, with boarded-up windows and a sense of strange magick, every bit of stonework here was bright and smooth, and the interior was lit up, the windows glowing, each room filled with stylish somebodies. A great deal of money and restoration had been put into it over the years.

The front door was held open to the night, manned by a guy with a clipboard and an older gentleman in full suit tails.

'Name?' the man with the clipboard said, looking me up and down.

'Um, I'm Pandora English of *Pandora* magazine,' I explained.

'May I take your coat?' the grey-haired man in tails asked as my name was checked off the list. He looked every bit the central-casting version of a butler. I half expected him to be called Jeeves.

Pepper's camera was slung around my neck and I took it off awkwardly, nearly dropping it as I struggled to get my coat off. 'I, um, have a pass,' I said, remembering to produce my media credentials. I fished it out of the coat pocket and slipped the red lanyard around my neck. The plastic tag hung down around my navel, declaring *Pandora Magazine – Media*. I put the camera strap around my neck and adjusted Celia's lovely black and white dress. The butler took my coat without a word. When I turned the man with the guest list was already talking to a glamorous older couple who had just arrived. I could barely see them beyond the white fluff of the woman's enormous floor-length fur coat.

I found myself alone on the threshold of the mansion with my media pass and Pepper's camera, looking anxiously to where Vlad had dropped me off. He was already gone. The uniformed valet I'd seen earlier was talking to a limousine driver at the kerb.

Well, here we go then. I turned on my ruby heels and walked into the mansion with an anxious smile plastered on my face.

Oh.

Wow.

The entrance led to a main room as grand as anything the Great Gatsby might have held parties in. It was cleared like a ballroom with only minimal furniture set up in the corners as sitting areas, where some of the guests reclined or leaned on couches and high-backed chairs, sipping champagne or brightly coloured cocktails. There was nothing as gauche as the thick rubber dance floor they'd laid down in the auditorium of my old high school in Gretchenville when the school dance was on. Here, guests danced to a six-piece band of tuxedo-clad jazz players on parquet flooring beneath four extraordinary chandeliers that hung in a line down the centre of the room. The exquisite space boasted a staircase at one end, shaped like an hourglass, the stairs seeming to spill down from the level above. An oval-shaped mezzanine circled the room, and guests sipping cocktails leaned on the railings to watch the crowd below. All around me people danced or stood around in groups, making small talk and looking elegant in their finery. The men were dressed in tuxedos or modern interpretations of black tie. The women were swathed in glittering jewellery and floor-length gowns in silk or sequin, velvet or tulle, some off the shoulder, others strapless to show off toned arms and fat diamond necklaces.

The dress code was not 'cocktail' at all, I realised.

I looked down at my pretty vintage dress and felt terribly underdressed, especially with the pass around my neck and Pepper's camera. Perhaps I should have asked about the dress code and come in something more formal? But just as I was lamenting my choice, a male photographer brushed past me in a black T-shirt and dress pants, a big camera slung around his neck. I relaxed a touch. *That's right. We aren't guests.* I was just here to document the guests. I didn't have to try to keep up with the Joneses, or whoever these people were. As if I could anyway.

Head down, I slipped into the crowd, sticking to the side of the room so I wouldn't get caught up with the dancing. I found a quiet spot near a staff door where people in uniform filed out intermittently with trays of champagne or hors d'oeuvres. I pulled Pepper's note out of my dress pocket and unfolded it. Names were scrawled across it. I read each one carefully. Thankfully, over the previous three months, I'd come to know a little about the fashion world in New York. I was no expert, but the famous names were at least vaguely familiar. If I didn't recognise someone, perhaps I could ask one of the staff?

'Oh, Mr Smith!' I said, spotting the famous knitwear designer Laurie Smith of Smith & Co. He was walking towards one of the groups of guests, but stopped when I stepped forward and touched his elbow. Laurie was a fashionable gentleman in his mid-fifties and tonight he had his long hair slicked back, and he wore jet-black jeans with a bow tie and smart velvet jacket. Luckily, he recognised me immediately. 'Ah, Pandora. How are you?' he asked warmly and shook my hand. A couple of guests observed our interaction.

Is that Marc Jacobs? Diane von Fürstenberg?

'Thanks again for the flower,' I said. He'd sent me a beautiful white orchid to thank me for helping with his supernatural spider problem. *I wonder how much he remembers?*

'Are you covering the party?' he asked politely, though it was obvious.

'May I?' I lifted the camera and he nodded.

Pepper's camera had auto-focus and was easy to use, and I snapped a couple of photos while Laurie Smith patiently stood still. Then he wished me a good evening, thanked me and disappeared into the crowd.

Maybe this wouldn't be so hard after all?

I seized the opportunity to snap a couple of the other famous designers, who acquiesced after having seen me shake hands with Laurie Smith. Or perhaps all the famous people here expected to be photographed? Either way, it was a relief to mark off a few of the names on Pepper's list. I moved through the crowded room, searching faces, but when I looked up towards the staircase I stopped.

Skye DeVille.

It was my boss, looking edgy and dark-eyed as she descended the hourglass staircase alone. She was even paler than I remembered, and tonight she wore blood-red lipstick and head-to-toe black – a long, slinky number with gauzy trailing sleeves and a plunging neckline. Something about her choice of wardrobe set off alarm bells. I hadn't seen her much since I'd caught her counting rice grains.

Oh, hell.

I instinctively ducked sideways through the crowd to avoid being seen by her and slammed straight into the back of a tall man in a tux. I gripped his strong bicep to avoid toppling over and the man it belonged to turned and smiled at me.

It was Jay Rockwell.

I took a sharp breath and it stuck in my throat for a moment. What was Jay doing *here*? Of course, he was in the magazine world. Why wouldn't he be invited? Perhaps I should have prepared myself for the possibility, but I hadn't, and now that I was inches away from him and unexpectedly hanging off his arm, I had to admit that he looked particularly handsome tonight. Jay was fresh-shaven and he smelled of a lovely, musky cologne. His tuxedo was perfectly tailored to his tall, athletic physique. Although technically, according to Celia, it wasn't a tux. My great-aunt had taught me that a tuxedo was usually something with a cummerbund or vest, whereas Jay was wearing a formal black dinner jacket and pants with a white shirt and bow tie. Whatever it was, he looked very good in it.

I let go of his arm and tried to think of what to say. Would he even recognise me?

'Hey there,' he said, getting the first words in.

I nodded, my heart racing. 'Sorry about that.' I

laughed nervously. 'Do you come here often?' I said, and then cringed.

Really, Pandora! Do you come here often?

'Well, yes, I do,' he replied, and laughed as if I'd made a good joke. 'Hey, wasn't that you at the Empire State?'

I nodded.

'Pandora, right? You were with that fellow in the Civil War uniform. Very clever costume.'

I smiled a little too broadly. *Oh goodness. Luke.* My heart did a little flip. 'I'm here to cover the event for *Pandora*,' I said, gesturing to the camera hanging around my neck, as if it weren't already obvious enough that I didn't fit in with the crowd of celebrities and wealthy New Yorkers. 'I guess you get invited to these parties all the time,' I said.

'Well, I should hope so,' Jay said, and smiled again, as if I'd been quite witty, though I had no idea why. 'What did you think of the view from the Empire State Building? Had you seen it before?'

I nodded. 'Yes. I love it up there. It's like you can see the world. Did your girlfriend like it?'

'She's just a friend,' he said.

Sure.

'Is that an accent I detect? Where are you from?' he asked.

Of course I'd told him all about Gretchenville before, not that he remembered. But in this crowd it seemed a particularly embarrassing admission. I hesitated and a whirl of black caught my eye as I realised that Skye was only a few feet away.

Jay noticed the look on my face and followed my eye line. 'What is it? Someone you're hoping to avoid?'

I shrugged. 'It's just my boss,' I said and tried to hide behind his broad chest, which was surprisingly easy to do.

He bent his head forward towards my face. 'Shall I whisk you away somewhere? Get you a drink?'

Oh boy. My heart did another little leap.

I poked my head around his shoulder. 'Oh no,' I whispered. 'Too late. Here she comes.'

Skye sidled right up to us and looked from my face up to Jay's and then settled back on me, somewhere just below my chin. 'Nice party,' she said, her gaze fixed on my neck.

The blood drained from my face.

'Nice necklace,' Skye said, and grinned in a way that gave me a shiver. One pale hand reached up for my throat and I jerked away from her.

'Is that vintage?' she asked.

I nodded mutely and held my hand protectively to my neck. I could swear she was eyeing off my jugular.

A dark look came over her. 'Shouldn't you be working?' she said.

'Pandora was going to get my photograph,' Jay said smoothly, covering for me. 'Or rather, I was hoping she would do me the honour. She's been doing a great job tonight.'

I raised the camera and took a shot while my boss sneered in the background, looking sullen. I never found her to be particularly nice, but she was far worse than I remembered.

'Well, I should keep circulating,' I said. 'I have a few more people to photograph.'

Within seconds a slim woman in head-to-toe red sequins appeared at my side. On some people it could look overdone. But on her, it was perfect. Her hair was slicked back to show off large drop earrings and to accentuate the plunging back on the dress. My jaw dropped a little. It was Pepper.

She certainly knew the dress code. I'd never felt so plain next to her.

'Hi, Jay,' she said, and those two words seemed a bit loaded.

'Hi, Pepper.'

I crossed my arms.

'A photo of the three of us?' Skye said, interrupting the surprisingly awkward moment. For one silly second I wondered if my boss would even show up on film, because by now I was sure she'd turned Sanguine. She had all the signs, I thought. But of course the photograph thing was just a silly legend. The undead did show up in cameras and mirrors, they just didn't normally like being documented on film. Perhaps Skye hadn't learned to dislike cameras yet.

I centred the three of them in the camera frame. I didn't much like seeing Skye and Pepper flanking Jay, with Pepper's arm slung right around his shoulders, though part of me was pleased Pepper was there to look out for him and keep an eye on Skye, who seemed a little dangerous. Skye leaned into Jay, pouting a little. It might have been that she was upset, or just that it was fashionable to pout. I couldn't tell. The flashbulb went off a few times and then I was off the hook. Job done.

'Well, I should get back to work. Bye then,' I said, nodding to each of them. With some reluctance, I left Jay with *Pandora*'s editor and deputy editor.

He sure was popular.

I walked through the crowded room, taking in the guests. When I reached the staircase I took a couple of steps up and turned my head and scanned the room, holding the polished wooden rail. At six foot six, Jay Rockwell was taller than most. I spotted him immediately. He was watching me go. We locked eyes and smiled at each other across the sea of people. I noticed that Skye had moved on, but Pepper was at his elbow. Jay had something of an amused look on his face, I thought. I offered a subtle wave and a closed smile, and forced myself to ascend the steps to search out the other famous guests I needed to photograph.

For the next hour I photographed fashion designers and their models and muses, a few actors and even a couple of rock stars I recognised but weren't on Pepper's list. It was an impressive assortment of guests, to be sure, and by ten-thirty I was exhausted and I'd crossed off all the names on the list. I finished up in a plush room overlooking Park Avenue. The light was low and the room smelled pleasantly of fresh flowers, a large bouquet of white roses set in the centre of a glass table. A couple in one corner appeared to be kissing on the couch – though I didn't want to look too closely – and a trio of guests I'd already photographed were chatting near the doorway.

I took a moment to lean in the bay window and stare out into the dark night, my fingers pressed to the cool glass. Vlad would be out there somewhere, waiting to take me back to Spektor. And Luke? Was Luke out there somewhere? Was he really possessed?

I took a deep breath. The party would probably continue for many more hours, but it was time for me to go. I didn't belong here in this beautiful house. I had to get back.

I turned from the window and started towards the now empty doorway, glancing at the couch as I went.

Was that . . .?

I stopped in my tracks. Yes, it was my boss. Had I looked more carefully I'd have recognised her trailing black gown before. I'd thought the couple were kissing, but . . .

Skye DeVille is sucking on some young man's neck!

I lunged forward and pulled my boss off the man. She was so shocked that she just threw her arms in the air and exhaled loudly.

'What are you doing?' the young man cried. He sat up and stared at me like I was a crazy person. For one terrible moment I'd wondered if it was Jay, but this man was younger than twenty-five – probably my own age – and he was shorter, too.

Skye straightened up and covered her mouth. I was sure I knew why.

I leaned in and squinted. Thankfully the young man's throat appeared to be intact. *Wait. Was that a smudge of blood?*

'What is your problem?' Skye spat, and pushed my shoulder.

It was not blood, I now realised. It was lipstick. Her red lipstick.

Oh boy. I am really going to lose my job now.

'I'm sorry,' I said, backing up towards the door. 'I thought I saw ... a spider. It was my imagination. Sorry. Bye.'

I scurried out of the room and down the stairs, heading for the front door before Skye could catch me and tear strips off me.

'Have you enjoyed your time at Rockwell Mansion?' the butler asked politely as I walked out, making a beeline for Celia's, making chauffeured car, which pulled up as soon as I hit the top step.

Rockwell. Mansion.

Oh, God. This was the Rockwell family home.

'Wait! You forgot your coat,' I heard the butler call out as I pulled the car door closed.

CHAPTER
TEN

On Sunday I woke to a golden beam of spring sunshine blinding me. I rubbed my heavy eyelids and sat up. It was nearly eleven o'clock, and the late morning light was coming in through a gap in the heavy curtains and hitting me with the accuracy of the gnomon on a sundial. My eyelids weren't the only part of me that felt heavy, despite the solid stretch of sleep: my body was leaden and my lower lip sat forward in a dissatisfied pout.

Jay.

Luke.

It's all a mess.

I found I had no desire to rise, preferring instead the safety and comfort of the old Victorian four-poster bed – the warm covers, the cocoon of the high canopy and heavy drapes Celia had recently had fitted. I propped some lace-edged pillows behind my head and barely moved for a long time, thinking. What had I done? My performance at the party at Rockwell Mansion had been an utter embarrassment. I'd arrived unprepared and made a fool of myself in front of the host – my evidently quite wealthy amnesiac ex-boyfriend. I had not asked enough questions of Pepper before attending and I had no one to blame but myself for that. Worst of all, I'd humiliated myself and my boss during an intimate moment. The young man she was with had been unharmed by her, though his ego – and hers – were likely bruised by my rude, ill-thought-out intervention. It had been red lipstick on his throat, not blood. What if I was completely wrong about Skye, anyway? What if she hadn't been counting that rice like I'd thought and she was in no risk of being Sanguine at all? What if I'd simply let my crazy life in Spektor spill over into my work life, clouding my judgment? Not everyone turned after contact with the undead. I'd even drunk Deus's blood and was assured it would have little effect on me – apart from a bit of a tan and that frustrating lack of resistance to his ancient, predatory pull.

I sighed and pulled the covers up to my neck.

And my friend Lieutenant Luke was ... well, what was he? Having him missing was bad enough, but now that I'd found him again those horrible green eyes of his haunted me. I missed him terribly, and the fact was, I didn't know what to do. Rightly or wrongly, it seemed to me that I'd had unrealistic expectations of him and the possibilities of our relationship. I'd pushed Luke into going outside the house. That had evidently been a serious mistake. Had we crossed boundaries we weren't supposed to? Broken some key supernatural rule? Was it all my fault?

On days like this I really didn't feel up to being 'the Seventh', not that I really understood what it meant anyway. (Why wouldn't anyone give me a straight answer? Why was there no course I could take? No proper textbook to explain it?) But one thing I knew for sure was that being the Seventh – whatever that was – would not pay my bills. A girl has to look after herself, always. My mom had taught me that. I needed financial independence, regardless of my great-aunt's generosity, but now I would probably lose my job, thanks to my own foolishness. Where would I find employment in Manhattan if I could not use Skye as a reference? Bettina and Ben's Book Barn in Gretchenville was the only other place I'd worked, and work experience like that was unlikely to dazzle New York's publishing types. What would I end up doing to make ends meet? I couldn't go back to having no lunch money and no mobile phone. I just couldn't let that happen.

Oh, Pandora, what have you done?

No, I was not feeling terribly impressed with myself. Not at all.

For much of Sunday I wallowed in icky self-loathing, the same negative thoughts cycling through my brain – *Jay, Luke, Skye, repeat* – as unhelpful as a broken record. I felt antisocial and I ate my meals in my room, though I didn't even hear Celia in the penthouse. The only company I enjoyed was that of Freyja, who curled up in my lap, furry, warm and purring, while I finished the last two hundred pages of the paperback novel I'd been enjoying. Unfortunately the ending featured the heroine running off with a romantic, blood-sucking vampire. Can you imagine? In my current state, that left me pretty disturbed, I can tell you. (*He's a killer!* I wanted to scream at her. *A predator! You can't trust him!*) I shoved the book under a stack of vintage *Vogue* magazines Celia had put in my room, as if not being able to see it would somehow make my very real paranormal problems go away. What I needed was escapism, but since moving to Spektor the tales that had once so delighted me cut too close to the bone. I couldn't even re-read Bram Stoker's *Dracula* without focusing on the obvious inaccuracies, and hearing Celia's frequent lament, 'That Bram Stoker has a lot to answer for.'

When the sun went down I did not seek out Celia. I feared she would ask me about the party. And most of all, I did not dare call on my once-close friend Lieutenant Luke.

In a very real way, I was more alone in Spektor than I'd ever been.

By Monday morning I was resigned to my fate. There would be no more pity parties from me. This was the day I would get fired from *Pandora*, but that was fine. Just fine. I would survive the humiliation as I'd survived so many other things. I'd worried about it long enough and there was nothing left to do but face the music, as they say. (What does that even mean? What music?)

I took the subway from Spanish Harlem, flicked a few coins into the upturned top hat of an industrious magician busking on Spring Street, and arrived at the office on time, wondering how Skye would do it. Would she scream at me in front of the rest of the staff? As she had before? Would I just get a letter? Would she take me into her private office and try to neck me, like she had that poor young man? Or rather, like I'd *thought* she was doing to him.

I held my head high and waved mutely to Morticia as I passed the big white reception desk. She was on the phone, but her big eyes followed me.

When I reached my tiny cubicle outside Skye's office, I took my coat off, placed the satchel at my feet, sat down and did a quick inventory of my three months there. The changes in my life since moving to Manhattan had been profound and I'd managed for this long. I could get through this. Skye was not in yet, but I was sure to hear from her.

'Where are the photographs?'

Pepper Smith had arrived at my cubicle with her palm out.

'Oh, of course,' I said, and fished her camera out of my satchel. 'I took loads of shots. I haven't downloaded them. Would you like me to—'

'I'll take those. Thanks,' Pepper said. She snatched her camera from me and turned away. 'Oh, and there will be a group meeting at noon,' she told me as an afterthought before walking away.

'Oh. Okay. I'll be here,' I replied. *Till then, anyway.*

So I was going to be fired in front of everyone. Great.

The next three hours ticked by more slowly than

perhaps any of my life. I sorted emails with little enthusiasm. Calls came through. I took messages for Skye.
I made a cup of tea. All the while, Skye DeVille's office
remained empty and I felt a heavy silence hanging over
the whole of the *Pandora* office, as if we were all waiting
for a ticking bomb to go off. Just before noon, the bell
finally chimed at the front door. I peered over the wall
of my cubicle, heart pounding, but it was only a delivery
man carrying a big cardboard box. He exchanged a few
words with Morticia, and then the deputy editor, and
made his way to the little kitchenette. When he'd finished
unpacking and installing it, we had a fancy-looking bright
red coffee machine.

Pepper wandered over to me, perhaps ready to fire
me.

'Have you used one of these before?' she said, and
gestured to the new machine.

I raised an eyebrow. 'Not really,' I admitted. 'But I'm
a quick learner.'

'Good. Read this,' she said, and handed me the
instruction booklet. It was written in sixteen languages
and it appeared much more complicated than the push-
button thing that we'd had before. You had to warm the
cups, grind the coffee, froth the milk ... I had a look at
the machine and the accessories it came with and, before
I knew it, it was just past noon – the hour of detonation –
and I realised that Pepper had given me new instructions
to learn, so ... Well, was I going to get fired or not?

I left the coffee machine and instructions in the little
kitchenette and joined everyone around Skye's office.

Most of the staff were taller than me, so I stood next to Morticia at the back of the small crowd, hoping to be invisible until the big moment came. It might have been my imagination, but it seemed a lot of us were tense.

'I've asked you all to gather here because I have an announcement,' the deputy editor said, and I thought, *Ah, here we go.*

Pepper had eschewed her usual skinny jeans and funky T-shirts and blouses for a smart green shift dress today, and she addressed the gathering of staff with one hand on her narrow hip. 'I have come on board as the new editor in chief of *Pandora*,' she announced. 'Our previous editor Skye DeVille is moving on to pursue another path. Pandora, you will now work as my editorial assistant. Ben, you are our new deputy editor. These changes are effective immediately.'

I blinked.

'*Wow*,' Morticia muttered under her breath.

I could not have been more surprised if she'd told us she was an evil fairy.

Come to think of it, with everything else I'd seen lately, that would probably have surprised me less.

It was nearing the end of The Day I Was Not Fired when the office door opened and the little bell chimed to tell us a visitor had arrived. Though it was probably a courier, I immediately sat up in my cubicle to check that it wasn't Skye DeVille, back to rip all our throats out for taking over the magazine she'd helmed. Skye would have extra fang for me after I'd pulled her off that young man at Rockwell Mansion. (That's if I was right about her being Sanguine, which I couldn't make up my mind about.)

But no. It wasn't Skye. It was someone equally familiar and infinitely more welcome.

What's he doing here?

Jay Rockwell strolled in, looking awfully good in his leather jacket and jeans, something folded under one arm. He leaned over the reception desk and spoke to Morticia, who seemed a little dazzled by his presence. They exchanged a few words before he spotted Pepper near the lightbox at the window and made his way straight over to her.

'Hey, how are you?' I heard him say.

Pepper seemed surprised at first to see him. She whipped her head around and when she saw who it was, her distracted auto-frown adjusted itself into something of a sultry smile. 'Oh, hi. I'm good. Great party on Saturday,' she said, and leaned one hip against a desk. She absent-mindedly toyed with a short lock of her fashionable white-blonde hair.

I ducked my head and buried myself in the papers on my desk, wondering what to do. I was Pepper's assistant. She was my boss. Did *they* have a history? Pepper and Jay? I'd suspected it before. But whatever was going on, I needed to keep out of it. It didn't matter if my budding relationship with Jay had been wiped away thanks to supernatural amnesia. It didn't matter that he'd taken me on my first ever real date, that he'd been so nice to kiss, that I'd basically saved his life. It didn't matter anymore. That was months ago and so much had happened in the meantime.

Keep your head down.

'Maybe we can get together again sometime?' I heard the newly minted *Pandora* editor say, and a little part of my stomach twisted.

Stop listening. Stop. It's none of your business anymore. None.

Though it was time for me to think about packing up, I found some more emails of Skye's to sort and then I felt a hand on my shoulder and I knew it was Jay. I knew it before I even looked.

I took a breath and turned my head.

'Hi, Pandora,' he said, and smiled down at me.

He remembers my name, I thought, and pushed my chair back from my desk. 'Hi, Jay.'

Jay Rockwell had something camel-coloured folded under one arm and now he lifted it up and let it unfold.

My coat. The coat Celia had given me. I'd been so flustered I'd raced off without retrieving it.

'Kingsley told me that this was left behind by a very beautiful young woman in a black and white dress.'

Kingsley. The butler.

'Oh, I ... um. Yes. Thank you. I forgot it,' I said, trying not to let his flattery get to me. My cheeks felt a touch warm and I worried I was blushing.

'I'm glad you came to our little party,' he said, with what must have been false modesty. The soiree had been anything but minor. 'It was good to see you again. Did the photos come up well?'

'Yup. No problems there,' I said. Pepper hadn't made any complaints.

I stayed seated, as if Pepper would somehow fail to notice that Jay and I were talking if I stayed in my chair. She did seem a little possessive of Jay, for whatever reason, and I really didn't want to get on her bad side, especially now that she was my boss.

Jay sat down on the edge of my desk, his proximity making me nervous. 'The party seemed like a great success,' I said, filling the silence with talk, though I did not care to mention that I hadn't realised it was his party, or his dad's, when I'd made those stupid comments. He must have thought I was a real card, coming to Rockwell Mansion and asking if Jay Rockwell came there often.

Idiot.

'What time do you get off?' he asked, taking me by surprise.

I swallowed.

Automatically, I glanced at the wall clock. It was past five already. 'Well, technically I'm off now,' I responded, with a fair bit of steadiness in my voice. 'But I have a real busy evening. Things are a bit complicated at the moment.'

An understatement. I just didn't feel like I could go on a date at the moment, if that's what Jay was asking. Not with everything else going on.

Though the idea *was* tempting.

'Maybe another time?' I offered.

Jay seemed to take my refusal well. 'No problem. I understand. If you want to catch up, give me a call,' he said smoothly. He pulled out a business card and wrote his mobile number on it using the pen on my desk. I hoped to hell that Pepper wasn't seeing this, though she probably was. 'I'd like to take you out sometime. No pressure though.'

Jay had asked me out before. Before taking me out for dinner in Little Italy. Before we got attacked by Elizabeth Bathory's henchwomen and I saved his life just a little bit.

'Thanks. That's really kind,' I said, and pocketed his card as quickly as I could.

Jay cocked his head to one side. 'We have met before, haven't we?' he said, squinting, some recollection seeming to come to him. 'I mean, before the Empire State Building. Funny, I just can't quite place it.'

I opened my mouth and closed it again. I didn't know where to begin with that.

'Well, I hope you'll take me up on my offer,' he said quietly. He stood up and walked away, leaving me with Celia's coat and his phone number.

CHAPTER
ELEVEN

After work I rode the subway up to Spanish Harlem and took my usual route through Central Park. As I walked I admired the green gardens, passing alongside trees budding with tiny, bright flowers, and I found that I felt rather buoyed. I even thought I knew why.

Yes, my life was complicated, but I had not been fired from my job (yay!) and, further more, I might even have a chance of a bit of normality.

I had a chance at being someone of actual interest to a *normal, living* human being – wanted by someone human, instead of being constantly put down and underestimated. And the best parts of my life didn't have to unfold strictly after dark, didn't always have to involve amulets and dead men and the constant creeping pressure of frightening prophecies and this title of 'the Seventh'. I could have something normal, too. A date in a crowded restaurant. A picnic in the sunshine. The things normal girls did all the time. Yes, I was grateful for my great-aunt and my strange gifts, too, but a little bit of normal once in a while would be very nice.

Perhaps Jay and I could even pick up where we'd left off? Or rather, where we would have left off had we not run into all that supernatural trouble. And Lieutenant Luke? Well, I didn't know what to do about my ghost friend or my conflicted feelings about him. The situation troubled me, but what could I do? I couldn't just sit around feeling sorry for myself. And he had suggested I see living men, before he became ... possessed.

Is it cheating to have one living boyfriend and one possessed dead one? And was I the only girl in the world who grappled with these sorts of ethical conundrums?

Addams Avenue was quiet as I passed Harold's Grocer, swinging my satchel and humming to myself, determined to be positive. Mist clung to the lit streetlamps and a few of the windows of the old brownstones glowed like rectangles in the thick darkness. As I approached Number One Addams Avenue I looked up at the tall building that I now called home, with its grand turrets and carved gargoyles, and I thought, *My life isn't so bad. Actually, it's pretty great.*

I could handle this strange world I'd been thrust into. I could handle it.

Grinning at the thought of Jay Rockwell, I put my key in the door and whispered, 'Please let me in.' The old door welcomed me by swinging open effortlessly. The lights in the lobby were off, and I absent-mindedly flicked on the light switch for the chandelier. It flickered on, the fixture askew. Its angle no longer surprised me. What had happened there was sad, I thought, but it was part of the Barrett family history, and history was important. Some people left an impact on the world. When they departed their spirits left a residue, or a physical presence of some kind. They leave behind something of themselves. And in my current state of mind that felt like a good thing.

I pulled my gaze from the cobwebbed chandelier and started across the lobby tiles towards the lift.

And stopped.

I was not alone. The woman in black was right in front of me, looking at me.

Or at least her black, featureless head was pointed in my direction. The black crepe widow's veil covered her head so completely that I could not see her expression at all, let alone whether or not she had a face. (I'd made that mistake before, communicating with other departed folks. It was best not to assume anything.) She was carrying the strange candle again and she turned and began walking away from me, her delicate laced boots moving silently over the tiles. She wanted me to follow.

'Uh, is that you, Mrs Barrett?' I asked to her back. 'Where are you leading me?'

The figure did not turn back or respond. She simply walked on.

Without even deciding what to do, I followed her instinctively. And then she walked through the hidden door beneath the mezzanine stairs. The one I had opened with the skeleton key.

I stopped just beyond the door and stared at the space where she'd been. Of course, I'd seen Luke walk through solid walls and closed doors, though he was usually very mindful not to walk through things when he was around me. (It can be a bit unnerving, as this incident quickly reminded me.) I realised it probably took a lot of concentration not to just pass through objects, if that was the natural, ghostly way.

When I opened the door she was waiting for me on the other side, her candle illuminating the way.

'The house seems not to want me here,' I said aloud, and though her featureless face did not move and she made no sound, I thought I could hear a voice in my head.

It is not the house, she said.

It is someone else. Something else.

Despite my fear, I followed her through the dank, twisting corridor. *Yes.* It led to the other side of the house — the secret side. I was sure of it now. Time passed strangely again. Did we walk for a minute or ten? And then I saw a faint sliver of light ahead. There was a closed door, light glowing in a thin line beneath the bottom edge seeping into the darkness. The woman in black turned, looking at me with that featureless face, and she walked through the door. Someone or something was on the other side of that door, lighting up that room, and I wanted to know who it was. *She* wanted me to know who it was.

Hmmm.

I put my ear to the door and listened. I could hear faint voices, talking so low I couldn't even tell if it was English. 'Celia?' I said loudly to the door. 'Is that you in there?'

No, it was a man's voice I could hear murmuring softly.

Deus?

I bit my lip. Perhaps I should just head to the penthouse? Mention what I saw to Celia? Being down here alone without a sword or even a torch seemed unwise. But that light was glowing under the door and I felt an almost irresistible urge to open it. I fished Celia's skeleton key out of my satchel and looked at it. Would it fit this door? I gave it a try and it slid into the lock with some effort. I turned the key, jiggling it around a bit where it was sticky. At first I didn't think it would work, but then I felt the old bolt slide back and the door creaked open on its hinge. Another secret room opened to me.

'Hello?'

This was a room I had not ventured into before. It was a study of some kind, with dusty books lining the walls from floor to ceiling. The light came from a tall candle that flickered from the centre of a wooden table stacked with journals and tomes.

The woman in black could not be seen. But a man stood in front of me.

Or most of a man.

'I see you made the acquaintance of my wife. You must forgive her. She is quite shy,' he said.

At once I knew who it was. My great-aunt had told me all about this man – the infamous psychical researcher and scientist who'd designed the mansion in the 1880s and lived and experimented here. This was Dr Edmund Barrett, who'd died in a mysterious fire supposedly caused by spontaneous combustion – a fire that consumed his body, or most of it, leaving only ashes and his feet. Yet here he was before me, with a pleasant look on his face, looking quite well, if a tad eccentric. Barrett was about five foot ten, and he wore a three-piece suit with a wing-tip white shirt and a slim, dark cravat, tied at the neck. A gold timepiece hung elegantly from his waistcoat. His hair was white as parchment, and it was clean but rather unkempt, as if he'd combed it back before stepping out into a windstorm. The effect was magnified by the presence of a pair of leather goggles with big brass frames, of the kind a motorcyclist might have worn – if he'd been riding a 1885 Daimler Reitwagen. The goggles sat on his forehead, just above light grey eyebrows, the leather straps flattening a thin strip of his wild hair on either temple.

And Barrett had no feet.

His form hovered steadily above the floor.

'Pandora English,' he said in a voice that was quieter than I'd expect. 'Please allow me to introduce myself. I am Dr Edmund Barrett.'

My eyes jerked upwards again. I'd been staring at the air that kept his legs up.

He knows my name, I thought.

He took a step forward. Yes, a step, as if he had feet where there were none.

'Don't come any closer!' I said suddenly, feeling the strange chill I often felt in the presence of supernatural energy, and death. There was something I didn't like about Barrett. Something terrible that put me on edge.

Barrett lifted a finger to his lips. 'Shhhh, you'll wake him,' he said quietly.

'I'll wake ...?'

Barrett looked sideways, seemingly to his shoulder, and it was then that I realised something was not right. Or rather, more was not right than I had first noticed. Barrett had no feet, but he appeared to have an extra nose.

At the back of his head.

Barrett flicked his eyes to his shoulder again, and I responded by taking very slow steps, walking around him to see what he was gesturing at. For his part, Barrett stood straight and stock still, urging me to investigate. 'It seems I may have picked up a passenger,' he said quietly as I reached his side, keeping as much distance as I could. I was backed up against a dusty bookcase.

Oh. My. Goodness.

Barrett did indeed have a 'passenger'. He – or it – was presently asleep and not exactly separate. Like Janus, the two-faced Roman god of transitions, doorways and time, Dr Edmund Barrett had a second face. At the moment that second face – actually it seemed like a whole separate head, or most of one – was sleeping. The head hung forward, eyes closed. What I could see of the terrible face was deeply wrinkled and withered, like a crone of a thousand years. Wild, dirty white hair hung over the features. I could not tell if it was male or female. I doubted it was even human. But it was certainly something powerfully sinister. I felt it immediately.

I tiptoed backwards and looked at Barrett with wide eyes. What could I say?

'Is he quite unsightly?' he asked.

'You've never met him?' I whispered.

'No, nor seen him.'

'Not even in a mirror?'

'We do not appear in mirrors, Pandora English.'

And Sanguine did. Go figure. 'When did – how did —'
I stuttered.

'I have travelled far, dear lady, to places you could not
even imagine. Places beyond the borders of the reality I
once knew. And somewhere in my travels, this one,' he
said, and flicked his eyes again, 'joined me. I don't think
you will like him when he is awake.'

'What happens then?' I ventured.

He shook his head gently.

The chill in the room was getting worse. My every
supernatural sense was on high alert. Each instinct I
possessed told me to leave that room, get as far away
as I could, but this was Dr Edmund Barrett. It was his
house. Who knew the secrets of the old mansion better
than he? Had Barrett returned to claim his home? If he
was still alive after all these years, was I merely a guest
here, with Celia?

Or maybe he was not alive, if his body had been ashes
and he was hovering like this in front of me and could not
be seen in mirrors. What *was* he, exactly?

'Have you been here the whole time?' I asked, backing
towards the door I had come through.

'Oh, no, no. I have not been to Spektor for one
hundred years.'

My eyebrows shot up.

'Pandora English, I have come back with a warning.'

I braced myself. There had been a lot of warnings

lately and I really didn't like where this was headed – or
two-headed.

Ha ha, Pandora. That was not even remotely funny.
I was so darned nervous. Part of me wanted desperately
to run out of that room and get back to the safety of the
penthouse, but Barrett? With a warning? I had to hear
him out. He seemed nice enough, though that thing on
his back filled me with dread.

'You have my skeleton key, I see. And you must by
now know the significance of Spektor? Of this house?'
Barrett said simply, clearly expecting me to understand
what he meant.

It was *his* key. Of course. Barrett had made a special
key for himself, so he could use all the hidden corridors
in the house.

'The significance of the house?'

I knew that this mansion at Number One Addams
Avenue was the epicentre, of sorts, of a Manhattan
suburb that did not appear on maps and happened to
be inhabited by an unusual assortment of residents. A
suburb that did not welcome strangers. A suburb that
was invisible to most people. Celia had informed me
that as 'the Seventh' I was powerful and would therefore
attract powerful forces. And I'd certainly done that. But
the significance of Spektor? Of the house? I wasn't quite
sure what he meant.

'You know the reason I built this mansion here?' he
pressed, waiting for me to make some kind of confirmation
that I understood.

My great-aunt Celia had told me something about

it being built in a way that helped focus supernatural energy, or at least that had been Barrett's theory in the design, supposedly. That's how she'd described it, though I knew nothing of the details.

'You wanted a house to live in,' I said. 'And a place to build your psychical laboratory. To do your experiments.'

He frowned. He did not appear pleased with my answer. 'Have you gone below the basement?'

Now I crossed my arms. My heels were at the edge of the doorway. The door had closed but I could just whip it open and run back to the lift. I'd be in the penthouse in minutes and increasingly, despite this perfectly civil exchange, I felt the need to do exactly that.

'No. My great-aunt Celia has warned against that,' I said.

Dr Barrett took a step towards me, watching my face carefully. He clasped his hands in front of him, as if in prayer. 'You really do not know, dear girl? Then I have more news for you than I thought.'

I felt a shiver go up my spine. I reached back for the handle of the door.

'Pandora English, you need to know that ...' he began.

I waited for his words but they trailed off and a strange look came over him. Barrett seemed frozen for a moment, like he was in the middle of a gasp, a breath he couldn't quite grab. And he just stayed like that, his mouth open.

And then Barrett's eyes closed and his head fell forward.

Oh no.

I pressed my back to the door, gripping the handle.

Barrett's arms began to move. They bent *the other way*, the suit arms folding back so that in the low candlelight it looked like his arms stopped at the elbows. But I knew what it was.

It was the passenger. Our conversation had awoken him.

Barrett spun around suddenly, and I stood frozen and terrified against the door, transfixed with horror. Here was another being entirely. It wore a suit, much like Barrett's, and I wondered briefly, implausibly, where you could get something like that, a suit with two sides, only this side was a bit tattered and undone, where Barrett had seemed quite impeccable. The being's hair was blown back now that it was awake, haloing its head like it had a finger in an electric socket. The tips of the white hair waved and swayed in the air. And this creature's face was positively horrific to look upon, the skin wrinkled and pulled.

And the eyes.

The eyes glowed green.

Luke, I thought.

He'd had the same green eyes.

Oh boy. Go! Go!

I ripped open the door and ran down the corridor, somehow finding my way, and up the staircase, not looking back. By the time I reached the penthouse, I was breathless and my legs burned. I hurried inside and closed the casket, and then the door to the antechamber, relieved to lock it behind me. If Sanguine could not enter the penthouse, what about a creature *like that*? Whatever

Barrett was, and that thing on his back? Was anywhere safe?

'Great-Aunt Celia?' I called out. 'Great-Aunt Celia?'

I rushed into the lounge area, skidding on the hardwood floor. Celia's reading chair was empty. The curtains were closed over the tall, arched windows and only the chandelier above me provided light, the crystals casting delicate shadows across the ceiling.

'Celia?'

I walked to the kitchen and found it empty, and then I noticed, last of all, that her fox stole was not on the Edwardian hat stand by the door. I should have guessed. She was out.

Somewhat reluctantly, I retired to my room with a fresh jug of water and a glass, wishing for my great-aunt's wise words, and even a cup of her calming tea. There was no one else in the world to share my incredible discovery with. Not even Lieutenant Luke, it seemed. For good measure, I pulled the chair out from the Victorian writing desk and hooked the back of it under the doorknob.

As if that would stop, or even slow down, any kind of nefarious supernatural being.

Behind the veil of all the hieratic and mystical allegories of ancient doctrines, behind the darkness and strange ordeals of all initiations, under the seal of all sacred writings, in the ruins of Nineveh or Thebes, on the crumbling stones of old temples and on the blackened visage of the Assyrian or

Egyptian sphinx, in the monstrous or marvellous paintings which interpret to the faithful of India the inspired pages of the Vedas, in the cryptic emblems of our old books on alchemy, in the ceremonies practised at reception by all secret societies, there are found indications of a doctrine which is everywhere the same and everywhere carefully concealed ...

I looked up from the haunting opening passage of *Transcendental Magic* by Eliphas Levi, and tensed. It was past midnight. I had heard footsteps and the door.

But of course it could not be Barrett. He had no feet to make footsteps with.

Quietly, I rose from my bed, where I'd been reading, still fully dressed. I crept to the door and put my ear to it, listening. I could hear the sound of heels on the floor. 'Great-Aunt Celia?' I said through the door.

'Pandora?' she called back.

Oh, thank goodness. I unhooked the chair and opened my door. My great-aunt was hanging up her stole at the entrance. She looked striking in a tailored red skirt suit with exaggerated sleeves and a thin patent leather belt fitted to the narrow waist. As always, her black widow's veil was in place. She regarded me with interest, clearly noting that I had something to tell her.

'I met Dr Barrett,' I said.

She cocked her head, that beautifully painted blood-red mouth of hers curling up on one side.

'Dr Barrett. Well.'

I nodded.

'He is back. And he is alive. Or perhaps not quite.' I couldn't think what he was, actually. In a rush I told Celia about my encounter with Dr Barrett and the thing on his back. 'I'm very worried. Is it safe here, in the penthouse?'

'The penthouse is very safe, I assure you.'

I stepped forward. 'Is it really? Are you sure? I know the Sanguine can't enter here, but Dr Barrett ... I do not think he is undead. He is something else entirely.'

Celia placed one hand elegantly on her hip. 'Dearest Pandora, do not worry. There is nothing to fear in this penthouse, and we can perform a protection spell to make sure it stays that way, if you like. Shall we do one now? Together, I think it will hold nicely.'

I raised my eyebrows. 'Do those work? What is it exactly?'

Celia smiled. 'Come to the kitchen.'

We went to the kitchen and for a moment I thought she was going to make yet another cup of tea. She put the kettle on while I watched her mutely.

'Get the salt.'

'Okay,' I said, and found the salt shaker.

'That won't be enough. Try the cupboard,' she said patiently, and I found a bag of flaked sea salt. 'There is a container,' she said, pointing at an empty water jug. 'We must mix up three parts water with one part salt.'

'With the boiling water?'

'The boiling will purify the water. Warm up the jug while we wait for the water to be ready.'

Once the water had boiled and then cooled enough

to be poured, I mixed up the water, carefully stirring the salt through. When the jug was ready Celia walked me towards the entrance to the penthouse. 'Now I want you to think about the word "evil", and what it means to you in this context. Think about who or what in particular you want to guard against. Hold the image in your mind for a moment and connect it to the word.'

I thought of that terrifying creature on Barrett's back, its wild white hair haloing those vicious, ancient features. And I thought of Luke, with those same strange, glowing green eyes, lunging at me ...

'Good.' Celia could clearly see by my face that I was focusing on what frightened me. The tiny hairs on my neck stood on end and I felt a little queasy.

'Now visualise the area you want to protect, the "safe circle", so to speak,' she said.

'Does it have to be a circle?'

'Traditionally it was, but in this case we can work with the area we have.'

'The whole penthouse?'

She nodded. 'We will make the penthouse our safe circle then. We will cast the spell, and as we do, you will remain focused on your intent – the forces you wish to block and the area you wish to protect.'

'Okay,' I said. I'd never cast a spell before. In fact I'd lived with Celia for a couple of months without even realising that she was a witch. (Did she even agree with that label?) The protection spell she described seemed surprisingly straightforward, if foreign to me.

'We will begin with the front door and move our way

around the penthouse, sprinkling the magick solution, and taking special care at the doors and windows. Remember to stay focused. Although we are not technically creating a circular safe area, we must connect our "circle", finishing where we started to seal the spell. We will go around the area three times. These are the words: *Thrice around and thrice repeat, all evil does this ring defeat,*' she said.

We stood at the double front doors of the penthouse with our jug of salt water. My great-aunt nodded to me and we began. 'Thrice around and thrice repeat, all evil does this ring defeat,' we chanted, side by side, sprinkling the doors with the salt solution. We progressed through the entire penthouse, from kitchen and hallway to the locked door of the antechamber, through the lounge and to my room, ending up back at the front entry. We repeated the ritual three full times.

'Thrice around and thrice repeat, all evil does this ring defeat,' we chanted a final time and stopped.

My great-aunt pulled an embroidered hanky from her pocket and wiped her hands dry. 'There. That's better, isn't it?' she said.

The jug was near empty. 'Will that really work?'

'Protection spells can be very powerful. Besides, you are the Seventh, and I am no slouch.' She held her beautiful chin high. 'Yes, I think this protection spell will hold nicely.'

'What about Luke? I don't know if I can sleep knowing he is out there, and that thing on Barrett's back could be controlling him somehow.' I was sure that's who was doing it, now that I'd seen those terrifying green eyes.

Celia considered my concerns for a moment. 'Let's have a look at your room again,' she said placidly.

My bedroom door was still open and we stepped inside. The ring of salt water had evaporated already, the spell set and invisible. My great-aunt cast her keen gaze from one corner of the room to the other, then tilted her head. 'What is that under your bed?'

'Luke's sword,' I said, and bent to get it.

'No, no, leave it there.'

I straightened.

'You are very safe here in the penthouse, doubly so in your bed with that iron spell protecting you. Keep the sword there when you sleep at night, as you have been.'

'Iron spell?'

'Iron traditionally gives protection,' she explained. 'It is why some people wear iron bracelets or amulets, sleep in iron beds or use horseshoes for good luck. That sword has kept you extra safe each night as you slept, whether you realised it or not. Keeping a sword under your bed is a traditional iron protection spell. Swords carry much power, so the protection you have chosen – unconsciously or otherwise – has the strongest magick. I dare say it is the most practical as well.'

She was probably right about that. A sword was a lot more useful than an old rusted horseshoe.

'Do you feel better now?' she asked gently.

I did. And I slept better knowing I was safe, even if the world outside the doors of Celia's penthouse was more strange and terrifying than ever.

CHAPTER
TWELVE

On Tuesday the hours at *Pandora* went by quickly, the office evidently energised by the internal shake-up. Pepper seemed to revel in her new position, and she was well equipped to lead, too. She designated duties to staff with a fresh directness, and organised aspects of the office that I hadn't even realised needed organising. New computer software was installed. Positions were reshuffled. Even the title font for the magazine was subtly changed, the alteration announced to all of us as part of another 'team meeting'. Pepper seemed real keen to make her mark without delay. And there seemed to be no resistance to all the changes, either. Not one person mentioned Skye DeVille, perhaps because she'd been so absent lately, or perhaps because I wasn't the only one she'd been unkind to. It was as if Skye were already dead to us.

In the afternoon I had some fashion shoots to organise for the upcoming issue and I had to put out casting calls to various modelling agencies, which I'd never done before. That was a kind of highlight. Anything I hadn't done before beat the constant grind of grinding coffee beans, putting the kettle on again and again, taking calls and culling emails. (I made no fewer than three Chai teas and four coffees with the new coffee machine.) And anything, I found, beat the idea of heading home. The closer it was to the end of the working day, the more anxious I became, I realised. Sure the penthouse was safe, if Celia was right, but what about the rest of Spektor?

For perhaps the first time, I didn't really want to go home.

What are you so afraid of, Pandora?

Sure, it was natural to be spooked by the apparent return of Dr Edmund Barrett, who seemed to have had a rather sordid history when he was alive and by my calculation had died a hundred years earlier. But it was not him that had given me such a scare, I knew – it was the thing on his back. I'd never seen anything like it, and it disturbed me deeply. What about the way Barrett had fallen unconscious just when it had woken? And he'd been trying to warn me of something, but what? What had he come back to tell me and where had he come back from?

I'd suffered aggressive bloodsuckers and armies of arachnids, yet somehow that creature on Barrett's back haunted me the most, with those awful green eyes – that and Luke's sudden change from the beautiful ghost I knew into a monster. It was the thing on Barrett's back doing that as well, wasn't it?

Hmmm.

At four o'clock I felt restless at the thought of

heading home. I placed my ballpoint pen in front of the keyboard on my desk and found myself staring at it. It was lightweight, but if I could really control it, if I could make it move even an inch, then I would have harnessed some of the telekinesis I supposedly had. *Mind movement.* Celia had convinced me I had the ability and it seemed I'd used it before without thinking. But consciously using it – rather than instinctively – was proving difficult. I'd made the skeleton key move once, but I'd thought my head might explode in the process. I'd been unsuccessful since.

Come on.

The pen was still.

I focused on it, my eyes wide, tapping my foot impatiently. I held my temples and squinted, my eyebrows raised. It was a good thing no one was observing me.

Nothing.

'Blah,' I exclaimed under my breath and gave up.

I sat back in my chair, twiddling the pen between my fingers and contemplating what to do. If I were to get ahead in this magazine I'd have to show some more initiative. Perhaps Pepper would be more receptive to my writing pitches than Skye had been? Though of course Pepper had basically stolen my breakthrough piece exposing the *BloodofYouth* skincare scam with barely an acknowledgement, so there wasn't a lot of trust there. *Hmmm.* I was feeling more than a little cooped up in Spektor, especially now that Luke was not ... Luke. Yes, this whole double life thing was hard sometimes. It all made me, much to my surprise, truly reluctant to hang around Spektor and explore Celia's mansion.

New York needs exploring, too, I reminded myself.

Raising myself up in my chair, I scanned the office, and on seeing that Pepper was out of earshot, I pulled out Jay's business card. *Should I?* I bit my lip and after another moment of inner struggle, I dialled his number from my mobile. (The reception was pretty awful in Spektor. Actually, it was nonexistent. So it made sense to call now. It wasn't because I was keen or anything ...)

The call was answered in three rings.

'Hello?'

Jay's deep voice made me sit up in my chair. 'Hi, Jay. It's Pandora. Pandora English.'

'I'm so glad you called,' Jay said, and immediately a part of me relaxed. *Of course, he hasn't been erased again. Of course, Jay remembered giving me his number.*

'I hope you're going to let me take you out,' he said.

'Yes. I am,' I replied, feeling more than a little guilty now that I was actually going to do it.

What about Luke? Would he mind? I felt like I didn't even know him anymore.

'How about Friday? Something casual? There's this great little restaurant in Little Italy,' Jay said.

Oh goodness. That was the area we'd dined in on our first date.

'Um, sure. That would be nice,' I said, wondering if I should propose another spot. Perhaps something in SoHo or Greenwich Village? The problem was, I didn't really know the local restaurant scene. And it had been lovely last time, after all.

'I could pick you up if you like,' he suggested.

I imagined Jay trying to find Spektor again. Not a good idea.

'I could pick you up from work?' he ventured.

I bit my lip. 'Maybe that's not such a good idea,' I said, thinking of Pepper's reaction. 'Why don't I meet you ... next door?'

'Next door? That's Evolution, right? The freaky store with all the skeletons and things?'

'That's the one,' I confirmed.

There was a pause. 'You have kind of a dark side, don't you?'

'Life has a dark side,' I said, and thought, *You have no idea.*

He laughed good-naturedly. 'Is seven okay for you?'

'Sure,' I said. Then I thought about hanging around SoHo until then, on a Friday night. It wasn't particularly appealing. 'Actually, why don't I just meet you there?'

'Or at my place? That way you don't have to worry about parking.'

Seven o'clock at Rockwell Mansion? 'Okay,' I said.

I hung up the phone and smiled. I'd done the right thing in reaching out, I decided. Why should I stay cooped up in Spektor all the time? I'd been in New York three months now. I had to make new friends.

And reacquaint myself with not-so-new friends, too.

When I left work I wasn't terribly surprised to find Celia's car at the kerb. My great-aunt was worried about me, it seemed. Or if she wasn't worried, exactly, then she was at least acutely aware that I was. I weaved between the throng of pedestrians on the footpath and into the open car gratefully, and thanked Vlad for coming – unperturbed by his usual lack of response.

Traffic was bad, and by the time we entered Spektor, the sun had given over to a waning moon and another stretch of night. As we emerged from the fog on the other side of the tunnel, Vlad hit the brakes suddenly, causing me to lurch forward, seatbelt straining. I looked up, surprised. In the headlights ahead, two figures crossed the street only a few feet in front of us, mist curling around them like smoke. Bones jutted out through gaps in their formal clothes, which were tattered to the point of dirty rags.

I gasped.

That shambling gait was unmistakable. These two were walking corpses – zombies of some kind – and the sun had barely gone down. We'd nearly hit them.

Dark magick is gathering, I thought.

I hesitated before getting out of the long black car at the kerb outside the mansion. Vlad opened the door and after licking my lips anxiously, I slid my satchel over my shoulder and scurried past him up to the entrance as quickly as I could, keys in my hand. I waved as Vlad pulled away, noting with some relief that the street just outside the house was quiet and the strange couple we'd almost run over had wandered off to some other misty corner.

I was about to mutter my usual welcome to the old door so that the house would let me in when suddenly the door opened itself, my hand hovering aimlessly at the lock.

Oh, hell.

A tall figure appeared in the doorway. Despite being caked with soil, this creature was terrifyingly beautiful. And smiling. She had her hand on the door.

Athanasia.

I grabbed a handful of rice in my pocket, my heart pounding.

Athanasia was wearing leather pants and a sleeveless top. I couldn't imagine choosing such an outfit for a therapeutic rest in a grave, but then I never had been able to figure her out. She was my Sanguine nemesis. Oh, hell, she was a *vampire*. The V word may have very negative connotations but it suited her from her fangs right down to her stilettos. (Which weren't looking so hot, I noticed.)

'Pandora English,' she said, still smiling. She wiped her face with one hand, pushing her filthy dark hair back. 'I'm so glad to see you. Please come in.'

I stood my ground at the threshold.

'You look ... better,' I said. The last time I'd seen her she'd had a face like dropped pie. With boils. Garlic was not kind to Sanguine skin.

A second figure appeared in the doorway next to her. I recognised her immediately.

'Skye?'

Skye DeVille was wearing the same long black outfit she'd been wearing at Rockwell Mansion. She smiled a horrific smile at me, flashing a pair of big ivory fangs. Her hands were dirty. So, Athanasia had called her when the time was right for her to rise.

Oh dear.

I swallowed. I'd been right about my former boss and that gave me no joy at all. At least I no longer felt bad about pulling her off that young man at the party. I'd most likely saved his life.

'Don't be worried. All is forgiven,' Athanasia said, and took a step back, welcoming me into my great-aunt's home with one extended arm.

This was a most peculiar scene – Athanasia and Skye just standing there, waiting for me to step inside, each smiling. I wondered if I'd ever seen Skye smile when she was alive. I doubted it. They both looked suspicious, though Skye was the only one with her fangs out, perhaps because she had so little control as a fresh Fledgling.

I narrowed my eyes, feeling the rice in my pockets. Thank goddess I'd remembered to bring some. 'So what's going on here, exactly?' I asked.

'Whatever do you mean?' Athanasia said in a saccharine tone that did not suit her in the slightest. 'Oh, you mean my new friend Skye? I believe you two have met.'

'Yes. We have.'

She kept smiling, urging me inside. Then her eyes flicked to something behind me and I whirled around, fearing an ambush.

'Who is that?' Athanasia said, seeming genuinely surprised.

It was one half of the zombie pair – the woman in her trailing white burial dress, her head slumped to one side. Under the light of the streetlamps I could see that there wasn't much left of her body except the skeleton that supported it. The woman – if that was still the right word for her – seemed directionless, drifting along the centre of the pavement on Addams Avenue. Her eyes were empty sockets, her fleshless lips pulled back in a deathly corpse grin.

'I think you'd better come inside,' Athanasia said, and suddenly I found myself agreeing with her. I stepped into the lobby and she let the door shut behind me.

'So everything is cool between us. No hard feelings?' I said, though I couldn't believe it for one instant.

'None,' she said, smiling oddly. And now I could see that the rest of Athanasia's merry little gang were in attendance – Blonde, Redhead and poor, sad Samantha. The two Sanguine supermodels gathered around their leader and their new pack member Skye, evidently doing their best to appear friendly. Samantha stood behind them, so still on those mezzanine stairs that she could barely be detected.

When my eyes met hers she mouthed the words, 'They're. Up. To. Something.'

Yes, I thought. *They are.*

I felt compelled to thank Samantha for the warning, but I couldn't without Athanasia spotting the exchange.

'Well, I'd better get going,' I said. I figured I should tell Celia about the couple outside. Was this a normal sight in Spektor that I'd somehow missed before? Though I knew the suburb had many mysterious residents, most of whom preferred to stay hidden, I hadn't seen or heard of anyone like that hanging around before.

I traversed the lobby and pressed the button for the lift,

not letting go of the rice in my left pocket. 'Bye then,' I said, and stepped into the old rattling lift when it arrived. I watched the Sanguine in the lobby through gaps in the iron lacework as I rose up through the house. They were all still smiling at me. All except Samantha. She looked concerned. It was a relief when they were out of sight.

Yes. They're up to something.

I watched the second and third landings pass, a cool dread growing in my belly. When the doors slid back on the top floor, they revealed someone standing near the entrance to the penthouse.

Or not standing, exactly.

'Miss Pandora English. The Seventh,' Dr Barrett said, and gave a little bow.

Well, isn't everyone friendly this evening. 'Hello, Dr Barrett,' I said.

The psychical scientist was in the same three-piece suit with that wing-tip white shirt and cravat, the brass goggles sitting up on his forehead. Behind his head was another one, I knew, though from this angle I could not see it. The doctor hovered strangely above the ground. He cast a faint shadow on the floor of the landing, I noticed, and he was not as transparent as most ghosts. *What is he exactly?* I wondered again.

Barrett had clearly picked up on my concern. 'Do not worry. I am here for the moment,' he said, though that did not seem an overly reassuring statement. 'I must speak with you.'

Reluctantly, I stepped out of the elevator. 'Yes, you

said something about that,' I responded warily, watching his eyes and keeping my distance. 'You said you had a warning.'

Barrett respectfully stepped around to give me space as I made my way to the penthouse doors and got out the key. I knocked, then unlocked the door and held my hand on it, propping it open with one foot, ready to leap inside if that thing on Barrett's back woke.

Dr Barrett watched me, clearly noting that he was not welcome inside. He brought his hands together, as if in prayer. 'Miss English, listen to me well. It is vitally important that you comprehend the significance of this place and the dangers lurking here,' he explained gravely.

I didn't like the sound of that.

Dangers like bloodsucking Sanguine, and green-eyed monsters, and ... what?

I turned and faced him squarely, despite my fear. 'Tell me.' *Tell me now before your eyes turn that glowing green, or just close.* 'Is this something to do with that woman on the street? She was like a walking corpse. There was another one, too. A man.'

His thick, bushy grey eyebrows rose. 'Oh dear,' he said. 'So it is already starting.' He looked both ways to see if anyone was listening, affording me a brief but grim glimpse of his passenger. 'Miss English, this house was built on an entry to the Underworld.' He pointed to the floor beneath us with one finger.

Now *that* was not what I was expecting to hear.

I blinked really, really slowly, and when I opened my eyes Dr Edmund Barrett was still hovering before me, footless and with a strange creature fused to his back. And he'd still said that we were at an entrance to the Underworld.

I swallowed. 'The ... Underworld,' I repeated with a long pause between my words.

I'd read about the Underworld of ancient myth, with Minos judging the dead and the nightmarish black Tarturus where the guilty were trapped, starved and tortured. I'd read of the beautiful green pastures of the Elysian Fields, where legend had it the blessed dwelled for a thousand years before their spirits were cleansed with forgetfulness and they happily took on new mortal bodies. Did such places exist *literally*?

'It is only one of several entrances, scattered around the four corners of the world,' he explained.

'I see,' I said, though that was an overstatement.

I'd read from time to time about supposed portals to the Underworld. There was a rumoured entry to the Underworld in the mountains of Spain, where hikers sometimes got lost in the fog and returned hours later, remembering nothing and believing only a few minutes had passed. And in caves on the Yucatan Peninsula, a labyrinth filled with stone churches and passageways had been discovered that locals believed led directly to the Underworld. And wasn't there a place in Scotland, in a hill? A place of Celtic legend?

'Each is difficult to find, of course. The portals like to remain hidden. That is how it must be. They do not wish to be found, except by the psychopomps who lead the spirits of the dead to their rightful place.'

Psychopomps. Guides for souls. It was such an odd word.

'You see, Spektor is a place of great significance,' Barrett explained. 'When I discovered the portal, I built the mansion here, right on top of it.'

Right. On. Top.

The entrance to the Underworld was what made Spektor invisible to so many. It was not the house, but the *place*. Or perhaps the two were inseparable now. It had seemed to me at times that the house itself was alive somehow. That it had its own will. My goodness, the sounds beneath the floor were coming from the realm of the dead? That was what was beneath the floor? Beneath those cracked tiles at my feet? Was Spektor some kind of pit stop between the realm of the dead and the realm of the living? Was that why so many spirits congregated here? So many members of the dead and the undead?

My head swam.

Yep. That was some kinda news, I thought. 'How many people know that this is an entry to the Underworld?'

'People?' He shook his head. 'No, very few of the living have this knowledge.'

And what about the undead, I wondered. Did Deus know? And what about my great-aunt? Had she been told? She'd told me the house had not offered all its secrets to her. Was this what she meant?

'Can I tell anyone?'

'Only those who are destined to know.'

What does that mean?

'And so, young lady, you can see why I had to return to tell you this,' he explained. 'The time the prophecy speaks of is approaching. You must prepare yourself.'

I nodded. *The revolution of the dead.* 'But how do I prepare myself?'

'Only the Seventh can know that, I am afraid. But it is vital that you realise the importance of this time, this place, and your role.'

I kept hearing that being the Seventh was important, but no one seemed to be able to tell me how.

Barrett turned his head suddenly and I flinched. Would his passenger wake?

'For now I must go. My wife needs me,' he said, and a chill went up my spine. 'She is the other reason I came. But I should like to speak to you later, if I may,' he added with a little bow.

'Sure,' I said. 'Um, I'll be around.'

He could not come into the penthouse, I figured. Not with that thing on his back. Our protection spell would prevent that thing from entering the space, and although Barrett appeared nice enough, that seemed like an awfully good thing, all things considered.

Dr Barrett turned and 'walked' away, moving on footless legs. At his back the passenger's head slumped forward, sleeping, the wild white hair swinging back and forth, obscuring that terrible face. When he reached the edge of the railing, rather than stop, he floated up over it and disappeared down through the house.

My jaw dropped.

I opened the door of the penthouse and hurried inside. It wasn't a moment too soon.

CHAPTER
THIRTEEN

hings were pretty uneventful on Wednesday and I was darned grateful for that, I can tell you. Skye DeVille did not show up with her new blood buddies to enact bloodthirsty revenge on all of us at the office, and the grind of the new coffee machine and the workload as Pepper Smith's assistant seemed to agree with me just fine. I spent the whole day sorting emails and taking calls, thinking about what Dr Barrett had told me.

An entry to the Underworld?

Could such a thing be real? Celia had suspected something like what Barrett had told me, but had not known for sure, she'd said. Yes, there had been clues – the cryptic warnings, the strangeness of Spektor, the way the whole suburb preferred to remain hidden. The sounds under the floor, even the sulphur smell in the stairwell. But how could I have guessed the reason for those things? There were so many questions I wanted to ask Barrett, so many things I wished I'd said. Yet despite his claim that he wanted to speak to me again, the evening came and went without his presence, so I didn't get the chance.

By the time Thursday night arrived I was champing at the bit, wishing there was some way I could call Dr Barrett as I'd once been able to call Luke, despite my intense dislike of the 'passenger' on his back.

I had to know more.

So it's already starting, he'd said, when I'd told him about the zombielike pair on the street. Had he meant that the revolution of the dead had already started? Or only the 'agitation' Celia kept talking about? I'd been so absorbed in Barrett's other news that I hadn't thought to ask him.

'Great-Aunt Celia, what should I do?' I asked on Thursday night. I sat on Celia's leather hassock in the lounge room of the penthouse, sipping the soothing tea that I was rapidly becoming addicted to. 'Dr Barrett said he had more to tell me but I haven't seen him for a couple of days now. I'm getting worried. There are so many things I wish I'd asked him.'

My great-aunt sat back in her reading chair. 'Well, you could head downstairs and see if he shows.'

I bit my lip. At the moment the thought of all those smiling Sanguine worried me almost as much as Barrett's passenger. What if Athanasia still wanted to kill me, despite the order that I not be harmed? What if she'd risen from the grave having finally outgrown her Fledgling OCD?

'Or you could rest up and conserve your strength,' Great-Aunt Celia said, in that familiar tone that suggested it was the correct option. 'As I rather think tomorrow will be more eventful.'

She finished her cup of tea and placed it on the silver tray.

'Tomorrow? Why?'

'Tomorrow is Friday the thirteenth,' she reminded me.

I hadn't realised. 'Should I expect some homicidal maniac to burst in on my date with Jay, wearing a hockey mask?'

She did not miss my cynical tone. 'Darling, friggatriskaidekaphobia is not entirely unfounded. But those silly eighties horror movies are quite another matter.'

'Frigga-what?'

My great-aunt crossed her ankles and brought one pale, slender hand to her chin. 'As you well know, Frigga or Frigg is the name of the Norse goddess for whom Friday is named, though some also believe it was named after our friend here, Freyja.' She looked down at the namesake of the Norse goddess of love, beauty and death – the one who rides a chariot pulled by felines. In response Freyja meowed and nestled her head into her furry paws again.

I did recall Frigga's relationship to Friday.

'Triskaidekaphobia is the fear of the number thirteen,' Celia explained. 'Hence friggatriskaidekaphobia – the phobia for this day.'

'But why are people afraid of Friday the thirteenth? Is it bad luck because of the Knights of the Templar?'

That was one of the popular views on why it was cursed, I'd heard.

'Because the last Grand Master of the Templars, Jacques de Molay, was arrested and tortured, along with a lot of other Templars?' Celia replied. 'Well, no. It was a bad day for them, to be sure, but the idea that it is the cause is a recent invention. Friday the thirteenth has always had a strong magick, since well before the Templars and their Christian army went down in 1307. Fridays have long been considered inauspicious days to begin new journeys or projects, even if few actively believe that now. Even before the "Last Supper", there has been a superstition that having thirteen people seated around a dinner table will end in the death of one of the diners. Twelve is considered a complete number – a full dozen, the signs in the zodiac, the hours of the day, months in the year, the number of apostles in the bible, twelve days of Christmas, the Twelve Olympians of the Greek pantheon, and so on. Thirteen, on the other hand, is the number of mystery. It has a strange, unpredictable magick. This dates back quite far.'

'Friggatriskaidekaphobia ... did I say that right? It's quite a mouthful. So tomorrow really is bad luck?' I said.

'Like so many superstitions, there is a grain of truth in it, but the true meaning has been lost. Did you know that so many people avoid doing things on Friday the thirteenth that it is one of the safest days on the calendar? No, Friday the thirteenth is not unlucky, per se, but rather there are certain powers at work on these special days. It can be either a lucky day or an unlucky one, but it is almost certain that it will bring surprises.'

I felt pretty unlucky at the moment, so I worried about which way my luck would fall.

'No,' my wise great-aunt said, perhaps again reading my thoughts. 'Tomorrow will not be unlucky, but my feeling is that it's sure to be eventful.'

CHAPTER
FOURTEEN

$\mathscr{I}$ had a little spring in my step all day at work on Friday. It would be a lucky day, I'd decided.

An influx of beautiful people came and went from the office through the afternoon, hoping to be cast for the upcoming fashion shoot. Some of the models were quite interesting to look at, with incredible Eurasian features, or blue eyes and dark skin, and some had tattoos. I helped Pepper manage it all, and I have to admit she was quite civil to work with. I was pretty hyped on caffeine, having sampled one of my own coffees, but mostly I knew I was just plain excited about what I would be doing after work.

Finally Jay and I would be going on a date. A real date that he would not have erased from his memory. That little thing, a simple date, was something nice and normal to look forward to in a world that felt increasingly dark and strange. Perhaps afterwards I'd have the opportunity to ask Dr Barrett some more questions, just outside the safety of the penthouse (that seemed best, all things considered), but I wouldn't worry about that yet.

First, I deserved this little slice of normality. And it was only hours away.

I said goodbye to everyone, and at five past five stepped onto the pavement outside the *Pandora* office. I noted the skeleton next to me, in front of the Evolution store, swaying on its joints, and something about it triggered a ripple of anxiety beneath my veneer of calm optimism. The sale sign in his bony hands caught the wind from time to time, spinning him around to look at me. The spring breeze had a bit of a chill as the sun went down, and I had my long camel-coloured coat from Celia buttoned up to the collar to keep warm. It was time to get going.

What shall I change into?

I had enough time to take the subway home but, sure enough, in seconds Celia's black car was there on Spring Street. It pulled up next to me smoothly, like a long shadow, and in no time Vlad had the rear passenger door open for me. I'd just *known* Celia would send him and that he would drop me off at Jay's place, too, when the time came.

The thought of returning to Jay's house gave me a little shiver of excitement.

'Thanks Vlad,' I said as I slid inside the car and strapped myself in.

The Friday evening traffic was even worse than usual but when we entered the fog down that little road at Central Park, I checked the time on my phone and saw that we were doing just fine. I'd have an hour to get ready, which was probably forty minutes too long, I was so eager. When we emerged from the foggy tunnel onto Addams Avenue I sat forward and gazed out the windows, searching for activity on the street. The lights were on in Harold's Grocer, as always. Mist clung to the buildings. The streetlamps glowed. All was normal – or Spektor-normal, anyway.

I noticed Vlad did not drive away when I let myself into the mansion. He would be waiting for me when I was ready to head to Park Avenue. Something about that made me feel a bit special, like I was going to a prom or something. (Except that my limo driver didn't breathe a whole lot.)

'Please let me in,' I whispered to the heavy mansion door, and pushed it open. I entered the cool lobby, satchel in hand, and saw that once again I was not alone. 'Hello Athanasia, Skye ...' I said, stopping just inside the lobby. I looked at the third Sanguine. 'I'm sorry but I never did get your name.'

The heavy door shut behind me.

My fanged nemesis, my former boss and the one I knew as Blonde were all gathered, posed elegantly around the mezzanine area, smiling at me once more. Athanasia had scrubbed up well. Her raven hair was glossy, now without dirt or twigs, and she was dressed in a stunning, skin-tight black corset and skirt, unsoiled. Blonde had evidently gone for contrast, swathed in not-so-virginal white. My ex-boss had raided their wardrobe and chosen something quite over the top to suit her new lifestyle – a fire engine red, lace shift dress with wide bell sleeves. Very 1960s Dracula's bride.

'Hi, Pandora. Gee, you look just great tonight,' Athanasia said in a particularly insipid voice.

Hmmm. 'Uh, thanks,' I replied. 'I have to be somewhere, so ... Well, you gals have a good night.'

All three of them nodded in unison. 'Bye,' they said.

I walked briskly to the old lift and pressed the call button. It was on the ground level and opened right away. The door squeaked shut once I was inside, and I pressed the button for the penthouse, noticing my new 'friends' wave at me as the elevator ascended. The sight disturbed me to the core.

Ugh, I thought. I almost liked Athanasia better when she was bitchy. It seemed more honest, at least.

The old lift rattled as it went up, and I absent-mindedly watched the landings pass, once again focused on the exciting evening to come. Where would Jay take me? Was it near the restaurant we dined in last time? What would our conversation be like? Had he thought I was joking when I'd asked if he came to Rockwell Mansion often? I'd have thought that was a deal breaker, right there.

It wasn't until I neared the top floor of the mansion that my guts told me something was very wrong. My stomach grew as cold as ice and the lift lurched, stopping just before opening on the penthouse level. Out of the corner of my eye I spotted the fourth member of Athanasia's vicious little gang – Redhead. I hadn't thought about it before but, yes, I should have noticed she wasn't with the rest of them. They usually moved in their nasty little pack, but here Redhead was, just a few feet away from me, leaning on the railing and grinning at me through the iron lacework of the lift. There was something in her hand: a piece of something mechanical, or a tool of some kind. Her fangs hung way out over her lower lip and there was something very, very wrong with her expression.

Oh no.

The lift lurched beneath me again and something above me snapped, loud as a gunshot. The elevator plummeted.

My hair went up, my stomach in my throat, as the elevator hurtled down to its destruction, taking me with it. The floors of the house whipped past in a blur. My feet rose off the lift floor and I reached up with both hands to keep the roof from collecting me.

'Stop!' I screamed at the top of my lungs, and a flash of heat radiated through me.

And everything stopped.

Suddenly, I was no longer falling. The elevator had paused just above the lobby floor and it hovered there as if I'd hit the brakes. And *I* was hovering, too. Though the lift had stopped falling my feet had not touched down on the floor again.

'Holy moly!' I cried, realising what I'd done, and suddenly the spell I'd cast was broken and the lift fell the final two feet to the ground, taking me with it. I crashed sideways in the iron cage, and grabbed the lacework of the sliding door to keep myself from slamming down onto my knees, scraping my arms. A thick cloud of debris blew up, cables and ironwork crunching above me. Dust spat out into the lobby.

Thank goddess the elevator didn't connect lower, to

the basement level. Still gripping the door, I lowered myself to my knees and closed my eyes.

Okay. So that just happened.

With some considerable effort, I yanked open the lift doors and stepped unsteadily onto the lobby tiles with scrapes up my forearms and knees that wobbled. The Sanguine audience was still there by the mezzanine, gaping, all having turned a whiter shade of undead.

Athanasia, in particular, looked positively aghast. 'She *is* the Seventh,' I thought I heard her say under her breath, and she brought a hand to her pretty, deadly mouth.

'Pandora!'

We all looked up. It was my great-aunt, calling from the penthouse landing. She'd doubtless heard the crash. In fact, it wouldn't have surprised me if all of upper Manhattan had heard it. At the sound of the mistress of the house, the three Sanguine snapped out of their shock and scrambled out the door of the mansion and into the night, scurrying like rats.

I stood in the lobby for a moment, holding my satchel and trying to process what had just happened. I noticed that the elevator itself had survived the tumble surprisingly well, probably because the fall had been broken rather effectively. It would nonetheless take a fair bit of work to get it operational again. Had the winch snapped? Or the cables?

Someone knocked on the mansion door before

opening it, and I stood wide-eyed as Celia's chauffeur Vlad walked in carrying a large axe that I preferred not to believe he kept in the boot of the car. Without a word he climbed the mezzanine stairs and chopped down the door at the top with the skill of a firefighter. A few minutes later it fell and my great-aunt emerged from behind it, with a torch in her hand. She walked down the stairs, frowning and surveying the damage to me and to her house.

'They tried to kill me,' I said plainly, standing beneath the crooked chandelier. 'One of them was waiting at the top ... she'd done something to the lift ...'

Celia closed her red lips into a tight line. Though she said nothing, I could feel the quiet rage coming off her. She would make them pay. Somehow. 'You are okay and that is the main thing. Come upstairs, darling,' she said, and touched my still-trembling elbow.

She exchanged a look with Vlad, who seemed to receive some sort of unspoken message from her. He turned and walked back down the stairs, carrying his rather terrifying axe, and disappeared silently into the night.

'The stairs are a disgrace, I'm afraid,' Celia told me apologetically. 'It's been like this for ages. Watch your step.'

Shining the torch ahead of us, she led me up through the house on the creaking wooden stairway, alerting me to steps that were rotting or had fallen away altogether. The wallpaper and wood panelling throughout the stairwell may once have been beautiful, but was now in need of serious repair, some sections missing, wallpaper peeling down in long strips. It seemed to take forever to reach the penthouse level and when we did we stepped onto the landing, puffing. I saw with mixed relief and anger that Redhead was gone. She'd scurried away guiltily, like the rest of them.

'That redheaded vampire – uh, sorry – *Sanguine* ... She was here,' I said, pointing. 'I saw her just before the lift fell. She had something in her hand, like a tool or ...'

Celia's lips went into that tight line again and something passed behind her eyes. 'Let's get inside and fix you up,' she said.

It took a bit of antiseptic and a couple of bandaids to sort out my battered forearms, but thankfully I hadn't broken any bones and there was not so much as a bruise on the rest of me. My brain, however, felt pretty rattled.

'I don't know quite what happened after the lift fell,' I said, running through the blur of events in my mind as Celia gave me a glass of refreshing ice water. 'I yelled stop, and then ...'

'And then the lift stopped falling,' my great-aunt said, watching me carefully.

'Yes,' I said.

Her right eyebrow went up, and then the corners of her delicate mouth. 'Well, you are progressing then.'

A melting ice cube popped in my glass and Freyja meowed loudly. 'Progressing? What do you mean?' I asked.

'Your mastery of mind movement is becoming quite impressive, don't you think?'

'*Telekinesis?* That's what that was? You mean I did that with my telekinesis? Is that even possible?'

She nodded. 'Whatever else could it be? First a sword,' she said, referring to that night on the roof, just over one month earlier, when I'd seized Luke's weapon to save myself. 'And now a whole elevator.' She patted me on the shoulder. 'You did well, Pandora.'

And I'd been worried that I couldn't move a pen on command.

Vlad dropped me off on Park Avenue at ten past seven, and as if reading my mind, he drove away before the door was answered, so as not to frighten anyone (axe or not).

Beneath my coat I wore a vintage, off-white dress my great-aunt had helped me choose for the date. It had a demure crossover neckline and long sleeves, and was cinched at the waist with a thin red belt, to match the ruby shoes on my feet. Celia said it used to be one of Ingrid Bergman's favourites, and it had the tailored, slightly padded shoulders of the classic 1940s designs she favoured. The sleeves, which were loose and closed at the wrist with three neat buttons, covered the scrapes and darkening bruises on my forearms. I had tucked the strap on my satchel inside it and was holding it like an oversized clutch hoping it looked okay. What I was wearing was what they called 'smart casual', so if we ended up somewhere fancy I figured I wouldn't look underdressed. (I'd been worried a bit about such things since the party on Saturday night.)

I took a breath and knocked on the door, and in seconds Jay Rockwell answered, wearing jeans with a smart collared shirt and leather shoes. He must have heard the car. He wore a dash of cologne as well, I noticed – the same scent he'd worn at the party – the party he and his father had thrown for New York's A-list. (I still couldn't believe I'd spent hours here without even realising it was Rockwell Mansion. Had Pepper purposely kept that information from me? She hadn't put him on the list of people to photograph, which in hindsight seemed odd. Or perhaps she'd assumed I would know?)

'Good evening,' Jay said, and flashed his handsome smile at me. 'You look wonderful.'

And so do you, I thought, gazing back and trying not to grin like an idiot. 'It's good to see you. Sorry I'm late.'

'Not at all. Did you park nearby?' he asked.

'I took a ... car,' I said.

'Would you like to come inside? Our reservation is for seven thirty but we still have a few minutes.'

'Sure. Thanks,' I said, and stepped inside Rockwell Mansion as he held the door open.

The grand mansion felt very different without the bustling crowd, the live jazz music and the flash of cameras. It was very quiet and even though the furniture in that magnificent main room was back in place, arranged elegantly, there was something lonely about the impressive space.

'Have you lived here for a long time?' I asked, following Jay across the huge Persian rug to a bar cabinet near the curved staircase. He had two champagne glasses set out, I noticed uneasily.

'I grew up here, and I moved back recently,' he explained.

'Oh?'

'I sold my apartment in midtown late last year,' he explained, and though he could have been living alone I immediately wondered who he'd been living with. Something told me it was an ex-girlfriend, or even a fiancée. Perhaps if I knew more about the New York social scene I wouldn't be wondering. It didn't seem like my business, or polite to ask, either, so I didn't press.

Jay pulled a bottle of chilled Veuve Cliquot from a silver ice bucket and I wrestled for a moment with what to do.

'Um, I don't drink, actually,' I said, intervening just before he popped the cork. 'But you go ahead if you like,' I added, though I knew people didn't drink champagne alone, as a general rule. We'd been through this before on our first date when he'd ordered wine. At nineteen I wasn't of legal drinking age. If we took a trip across the border into Canada, things would be different, though a night like this – a first date and an already eventful Friday the thirteenth (how had Celia known?) – didn't seem like a good moment to try alcohol for the first time, regardless of the law. Jay was six years older, old enough to drink what he wanted.

'Oh, of course,' Jay said, recovering smoothly. 'What can I offer you?'

'I'm fine, really,' I said, feeling a bit dull despite having just stopped a plummeting elevator with the power of my mind, an hour earlier.

Jay poured us both sodas with a squeeze of fresh lime and after a few minutes it was time to go. He pulled on his beautiful leather jacket and we left the mansion together, and when he opened the door his silver Ferrari was impossible to miss, now waiting at the kerb. The butler must have brought it round for us, I thought. This might have dazzled me a little had I not already been familiar with his car, and had I not myself had a stoically unbreathing chauffeur waiting for me while I'd got ready for this date. After the door opened upwards like a space pod, I slid quickly into the low, leather seat, careful not to flash the passersby on the footpath. The door came down and shut me in.

The drive was pleasant, as was the intoxicatingly normal small talk. And Little Italy was just as I remembered it. The streets were filled with glowing fairy lights and decorated with little Italian flags, restaurants nestled side by side, with patrons spilling out onto cobblestone streets to enjoy the turn of the weather – albeit still under heat lamps. Jay pulled up at the kerb and turned off the ignition, and it was then I realised we were right outside the same restaurant we'd dined at before.

It was like deja vu, and only I knew it had actually happened.

Jay hopped out and was waiting for me when the

Ferrari's space-aged door went up on my side. I held my leather satchel and accepted his hand. 'I hope you don't mind,' he whispered as he gently pulled me up. 'It can be difficult to get out.'

I didn't mind.

Jay gave his keys to the valet and cupped his hand at my lower back. 'I have the feeling we'll like this place,' he told me. 'It's low-key, but the food is supposed to be very good.' He escorted me up the steps to the restaurant, where the door was opened for us by the same young waiter who had served us before. The mouth-watering smell of Italian cooking filled my nostrils and I realised I was pretty hungry. I'd been so excited that I hadn't had much for lunch. Plus, holding elevators in the air with one's psychic powers burned a lot of calories, I figured.

'*Buonasera*. Welcome back, *bella*,' the waiter said, and flashed me a flirtatious smile.

Oops.

Jay frowned. 'Oh, you've been here before? I wanted to take you somewhere new,' he said, sounding a little disappointed.

'I like it here,' I said quietly, which was true, but mostly because we'd been there before – together.

The waiter helped me take off my coat and he left us to hang it up. Jay kept his jacket on. A few of the patrons turned to look at us – or to look at Jay, most likely, with his classically handsome face, dark head of hair and hazel eyes. The restaurant was packed full, every table occupied. Soon the maître d' came out. He was a short man with the round midsection one expects of someone who worked around food all day. I thought he seemed to recognise Jay, probably from our previous date, though Jay might have been used to being recognised. After the party at Rockwell Mansion, I had to accept that he was a far more prominent figure in New York than I'd realised.

'Rockwell for two. Seven thirty,' the maître d' said. 'I saved you a place at the window.'

We were led to an intimate table next to the glass frontage. It was set with a chequered red and white tablecloth, with a little candle in the centre, glowing in a red holder. The effect was romantic, if familiar. Cutlery was laid out, and a couple of glasses of water sat next to the upturned wine glasses. Jay pulled the chair out for me and as I took my seat the maître d' placed the menus on the table and left us.

Jay pulled his jacket off, draped it over the back of his chair, sat down and leaned forward. 'I'm glad you took me up on my offer, though it seems I'm not showing you anything new.'

'There's plenty I haven't seen in New York,' I said. *And plenty no one else sees.*

'How long have you been here?'

'I moved here three months ago.'

'Do you like it? Where do you live? No, let me guess ... SoHo? Tribeca?'

'Spektor,' I said, and took a sip of water.

'Really? Where's that?'

'Uptown a bit. It's not important.'

Jay absorbed my cagey response with a pinch of his brows, and picked up the wine menu to peruse the options. 'I hope you don't mind if I have a glass?' he said politely. 'I like a nice red with Italian. You're welcome to try it if …'

'No. You go ahead.'

Though I was old enough to save Spektor, and Jay's life, I was not old enough to legally sip a glass of vino, I thought darkly, once again fixated on that uncomfortable fact. Sanguine blood, though, was fine. What a strange world I lived in. I shook my head.

'What is it?'

'Oh, I was thinking of something else. Never mind.'

This was normal time – a normal date. It wasn't a time to think about my troubles in Spektor, or Deus's blood. And I had to pretend we hadn't done all this before. I had to try to relax. 'Do you come to Little Italy often? I mean, do you like this area?' I said, aware I was lacking some originality.

'I don't come here a lot. But I do think it's charming. This place came highly recommended. Is the food as good as they say?'

I nodded.

The waiter moved past and Jay ordered us a bottle of mineral water, and himself a single glass of red. 'Would you like anything else to drink, Pandora?'

I shook my head. 'Thanks. Water is fine.'

After a bit of an awkward start, we ordered a couple of mains. Jay told me about his time rowing in college, which I pretended not to already know about. I spoke as sparingly about Gretchenville as I could. It was not a big town or by any means glamorous. I was worried he would think I was just some small-town hick, but he seemed genuinely interested and nonjudgmental about my humble origins.

'Will you go back, do you think?'

'No,' I responded a little too quickly. 'To visit my aunt Georgia, yes, but not to live. I couldn't go back after ... everything.'

'Well, Gretchenville's loss is Manhattan's gain,' he said, and raised his glass.

Maybe, I thought, as we clinked our glasses together. I smiled at Jay and rubbed my neck absent-mindedly.

A basket of bread arrived before our meals. We'd both ordered pasta, naturally enough. Mine was angel hair with crab, which I'd always wanted to try. (You didn't get a lot of crab or fresh seafood in Gretchenville. Or Spektor.) Jay ordered a thicker type of pasta with tomato and spicy sausage. It looked to me like a kind of penne. I was somewhat more accustomed to ghosts and talismans than I was with Italian dining or pronunciation, so I'd pointed my order out using as few words as possible.

'*Buon appetito*,' the waiter said as he placed the steaming dishes in front of us.

We both tucked in and after the first mouthful I screwed up my face. 'Gosh, this is a lot more garlicky than I expected.'

'May I taste?'

After a slight hesitation I placed some pasta on my fork and put it in his waiting mouth, watching a bit too intently as his lips closed over it.

Jay chewed and swallowed, then sat back in his chair. 'Oh, that's quite good,' he said. 'Actually, there's not that much garlic in it. I was expecting more. You don't like it?'

Garlic.

The penny dropped. *Oh, hell.*

'Perhaps you'd prefer mine,' he suggested. 'Do you like sausage, Pandora?' Jay held some of his meal out to me on his fork.

'Umm.' After another moment of hesitation I opened my mouth and let him feed me a piece, flushing a little. We gazed at each other for a moment before I bit down. The sausage was very spicy. 'That's delicious,' I said, and laughed at my obvious awkwardness.

'We can swap if you like, though I think this one has a touch of garlic, too.'

He was right. They both had garlic in them. Of course. It was an Italian restaurant.

That blood of Deus's … What was it doing to me?

'No, mine is fine,' I insisted. I'd eat sparingly and hope I didn't come up in hives or some darned thing. 'Did you enjoy your party on Saturday?' I asked Jay to change the subject.

'My dad throws it every year. I guess it's kind of fun.'

'But?'

He hesitated. 'But … I don't know. It's kind of stuffy for me. Sometimes I'd prefer something a little less formal.' He took another bite of his pasta. 'You know, it may sound clichéd to say this, but …' He smiled to himself. 'No.'

'Go ahead. What?' I took another bite, trying to ignore

the odd sensation of the garlic on my tongue.

'It's strange, but though I've only just met you, I feel like I've known you before.'

I choked.

'Are you okay?'

'I'm fine. Just fine.' I took a sip of water to help the mouthful of pasta go down.

Something dark sailed past the window and I stiffened. That strange, cold feeling came over my belly. But though I scanned the street outside the window, I couldn't see anything out of the ordinary.

Jay noticed my changed expression instantly. 'Are you okay?'

'Sorry. Yeah, I'm fine.' I licked my lips and flicked my eyes to the window again. 'Thanks.'

'Is the crab okay for you? We can swap if you like. Or we can order you something else?'

My plate was still quite full. 'It is really lovely,' I said truthfully. The dish was one of the best I'd tasted, or would have been if it wasn't for my unexpected issue with garlic. But I suddenly wasn't feeling hungry at all.

That feeling in my belly. That cold dread.

There was the sound of the front door opening and closing, and a collective murmur rippled through the restaurant, a jolt of awareness that went through each diner at the tables, followed soon after by a conspicuous silence. When Jay and I looked up to see what had caused it, I simply could not comprehend what I was seeing.

A dark figure had arrived at our table.

'Excuse me, Miss Pandora English. I am sorry to

disturb you, but your presence is required urgently.'

Deus.

He was impeccably groomed, long-lashed and magnetically beautiful to look upon, and I swore every person in the restaurant – male and female – was doing just that, staring at him, open-mouthed. Despite the urgency of his words, Deus had that eternal Kathakano smile on his face and it seemed impossible that anything could be so important that he needed to disturb my perfectly normal, perfectly nice date like this, smiling at me and telling me my presence was required elsewhere.

'It can't wait until tomorrow?' I ventured, trying not to sound put out. It was quite unprecedented for me to see Deus outside the mansion. In fact, I realised I had never seen him outside the confines of Celia's antechamber. (The time on the roof didn't count because I hadn't seen him at all.)

'I'm afraid it is quite urgent,' Deus replied, his dark gaze seeming to speak to me.

After a moment I managed to break from his gaze to notice my date's expression, which was one of surprise and jealousy. *Who is this man? How does he know Pandora?* I could imagine him wondering.

'It is quite important,' I told him, though I had no idea what could be so important that it couldn't wait until I got home. I sure hoped it had nothing to do with those Sanguine troublemakers who'd already had a fair stab at ruining my evening.

'I'm so sorry. I will make it up to you, I promise. Can I call you tomorrow?' I said to Jay.

'If you must go, I understand,' he said diplomatically, and stood.

He got the attention of our waiter, who he asked to bring my coat and his car. Actually, we already had everyone's attention, so it wasn't much of an effort. Jay and Deus walked me to the door and stood side by side as we waited, not exchanging a word. Jay towered over both of us and he seemed to stand particularly tall, chest out. He was more than half a foot taller than the powerful Sanguine. The waiter brought my coat and Jay helped me into it and gave me a quick, slightly possessive kiss. He and Deus exchanged a long, hard look while I buttoned up my coat, Jay apparently trying to size up the older man. Of course, he could have no idea just *how much* older Deus was.

'I'm so sorry for this,' I told Jay again.

I stood on tiptoe to plant a quick kiss on his cheek and walked out of the restaurant with the ancient Kathakano Sanguine at my side.

CHAPTER
FIFTEEN

$\mathcal{I}$ stood outside the service entrance for the restaurant in Little Italy with my arms tightly crossed hugging my satchel. The entrance was in a narrow alley paved with old cobblestones and it hadn't been easy to negotiate in the dark. Inside, Jay Rockwell was probably settling the bill and wondering why in the world he'd bothered to take me out. I should have at least put some money on the table to cover the meal, but I hadn't thought of it in time. I might have also said something about Deus being a friend of my great-aunt's, but it was too late now.

'What is so important that it couldn't wait?' I asked Deus, feeling a bit proud of myself for not completely succumbing to his Sanguine magnetism. Still, I had come out here to a dark alley with barely a thought for why, or for my own safety.

'Pandora, please get on my back,' Deus said.

'Pardon me?'

'Miss Pandora, I implore you. Please get on my back. Or permit me to embrace you,' he urged.

'I most certainly will not,' I protested, and took a step away from him. I shouldn't have left the restaurant at all. What was I thinking, leaving Jay like that? What kind of Sanguine trickery was this?

'Do not trifle with me. There is no time,' Deus said, and seized me so suddenly it took my breath away. His hard arms locked tightly around me – an embrace so steely I could not break it using all my strength. 'Just try to relax. You are perfectly safe with me,' he assured me.

And we shot into the air.

We must have been a hundred feet above the restaurant before I dared to open my eyes. We had left the ground so quickly I felt like my stomach was still down in the alley. I looked past my shoes – which now dangled without a foothold hundreds of feet in the air – and saw the lights of Little Italy grow smaller by the second, the low rooftops fading away. I spotted the illuminated strip of green trees by the Grand Street Metro. The lights of Chinatown. The Brooklyn Bridge. The air whistled past my ears and my mouth opened and closed a few times, but nothing came out.

I was glad I hadn't eaten a whole lot.

Once we'd reached a truly dizzying height, Deus flew us uptown, our bodies sailing sideways, his over the top of mine. I watched the stars and the night clouds race past above us as I held on for my life. I shut my eyes again.

Don't vomit.

Don't.

'Can you hear me, Pandora English?' Deus asked.

I nodded, my eyes closed tightly. His face was inches from mine. Despite the wind roaring in my ears, I could hear him just fine.

'There is a powerful necromancer loose in Manhattan. He must be stopped.'

'A necromancer?' I shouted.

'There,' Deus announced, and pointed down, holding me with one strong arm as we continued through the air at a heart-stopping pace.

I did not much like this change of grip. It made me hold on to him even more tightly, my knuckles white. Deus turned in the air, pulling me upright, and as the earth came into view again I saw that the most extraordinary scene was unfolding on a street in lower midtown, where cars were stopped and a group of people were gathered, circled by a strange, glowing green mist. The mist shifted, tendrils reaching out and flicking back like the arms of some tentacled sea creature. We flew closer, and I saw a familiar figure in the centre of the mad scene. It was Dr Barrett, or rather his passenger. The creature on Barrett's back had its arms raised and was shrieking in an unintelligible language, manipulating the swirling mist with the grand movements of a conductor.

We swooped past and to my horror I saw that the necromancer was, somehow, pulling corpses from the street like they were weeds. Bodies burst through the grass on the median strips, or straight from the pavement, and swayed on bony legs.

By now a dozen skeletons were following Barrett down Second Avenue, shuffling and moaning.

'Where are they all coming from?' I shouted. They were coming right out of the ground and I could see no graveyards nearby.

'Every major city has bodies buried beneath the streets in unmarked graves. Most have been there for a very, very long time,' Deus explained as I held him.

I guess Deus would know. He may have even put some of them there.

'How does he know where to find them? What is that green mist?' I asked.

'It is the necromancer's spell, Pandora. Only you can see it, but I can feel it. I cannot get too close to this necromancer or he'll have me under his control.'

Like Luke.

Luke was under the necromancer's spell. Those green eyes had been like the necromancer's, had been the colour of that strange mist. And now I was sure Barrett's passenger had been the reason for that couple shuffling through Spektor, risen from the grave . . .

'Where is Celia?' I asked, panicked. I needed to ask her what to do. We needed her help.

'Your great-aunt is at the mansion, holding them back. She cannot help us.'

'She's holding who back?'

'The dead,' Deus shouted against the wind. 'She has created a spell to keep them at bay, but if the necromancer comes back he will be too powerful for her. I fear the protection spell will not hold. If they succeed in opening the portal, reuniting the spirits of the dead with their bodies, the revolution of the dead will begin.'

The revolution of the dead, I thought. *It's real.*

'You need to stop him, Pandora English.'

I gaped, still holding on tight. '*I* need to?! But how?'

'You are the Seventh. You have the power of necromancy, Pandora English. Use it.' Deus flew towards the ground, landing a block or two away from the reach of the tendrils of green mist.

'But I don't know how!' I protested as he set me down. 'I don't know what to do.'

I stood a little unsteadily on jittery legs on the pavement, and looked around me. Somehow, strangers passed us on the footpath as if they hadn't even noticed our quite unconventional arrival. They seemed to not even see us.

Deus took my hand in his. It was cold. 'I'm sorry I must leave you here. I cannot stay. I must keep clear of the spell. I'll be watching from above and I'll do what I can,' he told me, and before I could respond he shot up into the air again in a rush of black, like the flapping of dark wings.

I blinked.

This was the East Village – the street sign next to me said 'E. Houston'. I turned and jogged in the direction of the mist, dodging and weaving between pedestrians, realising with some fascination that everyone appeared to be going about their evening routines as if nothing were wrong. 'Humans reject the supernatural,' Celia had told me. 'They are blind to it.' But how could they be *that* blind? We'd fallen out of the sky! There was a swirling green mist on Second Avenue! Even if they could not see the spell and the corpses, as I could, couldn't they hear the shrieking?

But by the time I reached Second Avenue the mist was gone and it was quiet – too quiet – particularly for nine o'clock on a Friday night. Cars rolled past slowly, far below the speed limit, wheels crunching on the road as they passed. Through the windshield of a Cadillac I spotted the vacant, open-mouthed expression of a driver as she gripped the wheel, her car trundling past in odd fits and starts. Others rolled as if the engines were off, moving almost without sound. They moved so slowly I could probably have walked out between the vehicles without being hit. A couple shuffled past me on the footpath – a man in a suit and a woman in jeans and a trench coat, holding hands. At first I thought they were zombies, they moved so slowly and their faces were so slack, but their clothes were clean, their skin untouched by decay. I looked into their eyes, from one to the other and back again. They were glazed over. Both of them. I stood to one side to let them pass.

Far above, I saw a dark shape move across the night sky.

A shriek rang out and I snapped my head around. Down the street in the other direction I caught a glimpse of the peculiar mist as one green tendril flicked out across the pavement and disappeared again. Against my better instincts I ran towards it, wishing for all the world that I was someone who could flee the other way, not someone who was inexplicably caught up in all this, responsible for putting a stop to it – responsible enough that a powerful

vampire had plucked me from a restaurant in Little Italy
to enlist my help.

How did my boring little life lead me here? To this?

And how the coldness in my belly ached. The closer
I got to where I'd seen the flash of mist, the worse it
was. Whatever the necromancer was up to in this part
of town, the dread in my belly told me it was very, very
bad. I turned up a narrow alley and saw the green mist
waving in the air like luminescent seaweed, just past an
old stone wall. I squinted. 'New York Marble Cemetery',
a sign said.

Oh boy. So that's it.

This was Manhattan's first non-secular burial ground,
a deceptively simple-looking half-acre lawn above one
hundred and fifty-six underground Tuckahoe marble
burial vaults, famously built at a time when traditional
burials in coffins were outlawed due to concerns about
the outbreaks of yellow fever. It was believed that the
sealed vaults could prevent contagion from the supposed
miasma emitted by corpses. Hundreds were interred here
in the 1800s, though some were later moved. How many
were there now?

The old cemetery looked like a small park or secret
garden with crumbling stone walls, if you didn't take a
closer look. By the time I caught up with Barrett and his
passenger, they were in the middle of the cemetery on
the other side of the two wrought-iron gates, which they
appeared to have broken.

And he/it/they were not alone.

Skeletal creatures paced the cemetery, moaning and

turning in circles. Two dozen of them at least. Most were centuries old but two of them were more recently dead, raw flesh and gore still hanging off them, their clothing dishevelled or torn away. Had he pulled them from a nearby morgue? From an accident? I shuddered to think.

'*Ahhhhheeeeeeeekkkkkkk!*'

I stood by the gates and covered my ears as a terrible shrieking filled the air, loud enough to ... well, wake the dead. And I supposed that was precisely what it was for.

The shrieking from Barrett's necromancer was so high-pitched and so unnatural a tone that I thought my eardrums would bleed. Each of the zombies had also joined in the blood-curdling chorus, rousing the remaining dead beneath them. I covered my ears with my hands. Mercifully the shrieking stopped after less than a minute, and I uncovered my ears. There was a brief, blessed silence, but then I heard moaning, and muffled voices rose up through the dead earth. The words were not clear, yet it was apparent to me that dozens upon dozens of souls were waking from their deep slumbers in the vaults below. I wondered if the living residents of Manhattan could hear it? The shrieking? The moaning?

Then came the knocking. The pounding against marble.

The ground began to move. Something shifted beneath me and I stumbled backwards.

A hand shot up through the dirt.

Then another.

Pure terror threatened to overcome me.

Think, Pandora.

The shrieking began again and I covered my ears, trying to clear my head. All around me the green mist circled and the crowd of corpses walked through the cemetery, agitated and agitating for more company, apparently unaware of or unmoved by my presence.

Do something!

Dr Edmund Barrett's head hung down limply, the scientist evidently quite unconscious as the necromancer on his back pulled at the earth with invisible strings, the green mist coiling in the air and coating the lawn in an eerie, glowing carpet. How long had he been unconscious? I wondered. How long had his passenger been in control?

The old cemetery continued to come to life, the dead knocking and breaking against the marble tombs deep in the ground. I danced across the grass, trying to keep clear of the bony fingers shooting up through the dirt. The cemetery's residents – New Yorkers of the eighteenth and nineteenth centuries – were stripped to the bone, their muscles long since decayed to dirt, yet they were charged with enough unnatural power to break through the earth and climb unsteadily to their feet, or what was left of them, their burial clothes in tatters or rotted away to nothing, soil dripping off them like dark cremation dust. Who knew what they were capable of.

'Go back!' I shouted to them. 'Go back to your resting places!'

My words meant nothing to them. The necromancer had willed them on their unspoken mission, and now that hundreds of them had risen, the skeletal figures began a slow death march out of the broken cemetery gates and onto the street, animated by the glowing green mist swirling at their feet. The necromancer floated before them, leading the march. I turned and watched them, horrified and feeling useless, while behind me, even more corpses continued to rise.

And now there was a living crowd, too, I realised. Groups of stunned New Yorkers screamed or stood gaping. How on earth would they explain what they were seeing?

'Stop! I command you!' I finally screamed, and the obsidian ring on my finger grew warm.

I was onto something.

'I *command* you!' I repeated. 'I command you to return to your graves!'

I held the ring out and concentrated until the veins in my forehead pounded. The obsidian ring grew hotter and hotter until I almost couldn't bear it. Eventually the walking dead stopped in their tracks. And they turned – two hundred of them, maybe more – and fixed their hollow eye sockets on me.

This was the moment, I realised. Either the necromancer would command them to tear me limb from limb, or ...

'As the Seventh, I *command* you to return to your graves!' I declared, one arm raised in a fist.

There was a shocking flash of light, and the obsidian ring burned so hot I fell to my knees and held my wrist, resisting the urge to pull the ring from my finger. But the dead who had stopped at the gates began to move again. They began to retreat, walking right past me and crawling back into the ground from whence they came.

It's working!

I stood up and repeated my command. Again the ring burned, and I gritted my teeth. But it was working.

The zombies disappeared back into the disturbed ground of the cemetery, slipping into the broken earth like it was quicksand, some feet first, others on their bony hands and knees. Gradually, the earth closed in around them, as if patted down by invisible hands, the grass moving back into place. I continued my commands until the cemetery was still, the green mist fading away.

Wow. I did that?

Now the necromancer was at the gates, hovering over the ground, green eyes glowing with silent rage. Finally – unfortunately – it had turned its focus on me, and I felt that awful black magick. The tips of my hair began to rise, as if with static shock. I took a step backwards. Then another.

'Dr Barrett, wake up!' I yelled, panicked. 'If you're in there, wake up now! Please!'

The creature opened his arms, fingers spread like claws, and let out a ghastly, furious wail. He threw his arms forward suddenly, as if tossing something, and I was hit with a wall of cold, foul-smelling air that blew my hair back and lifted me right off the ground. The force of it winded me and I fell backwards and crumpled into a ball, head first, striking the hard earth with a crunch. When I got to my feet again, disoriented, the necromancer had already vanished and I saw a wisp of green mist disappear over the cemetery walls.

All was silent around me.

The residents of New York Marble Cemetery had returned to their graves. The spell that had animated them was now absent, and the mist had left with it. I breathed a sigh of deep relief and brought my hands to my head, which ached from the fall. I allowed myself to sit down on the cold grass for a moment, catching my breath. My coat from Celia was grass-stained, and I'd lost my satchel somewhere in all the madness, I now realised. Had I even had it when Deus set me down on the street? And my hand hurt badly, too.

But I did it.

I'd actually commanded the dead, just as Deus said I could. I was about to congratulate myself when there was another ear-piercing shriek, some distance away.

Oh, hell.

There was evidently no time to rest. I got up and ran out through the broken gates, down the alley and into the street. I took only a moment to note that the living humans on Second Avenue had dispersed, walking away from the scene with strange, shuffling slowness – what was wrong with them? – then I rushed as fast as I could towards the strange, glowing mist which had gathered again a mere block away.

And when I saw where it was, I thought, *You have to be kidding me.*

It was another marble cemetery, beyond high black gates. I'd forgotten that New York Marble Cemetery, where I had just fought to return the dead to their graves, was very near the similarly named New York *City* Marble Cemetery. It had been built only one year after the first cemetery – and it was larger. With more dead.

This was bad news. Very bad. I could not dash around the entire island of Manhattan, trying to keep the dead in their graves. My skin was already red with burns under the obsidian ring Celia had given me – a ring that had belonged to my great-great-grandmother, the fortune teller Madame Aurora. 'It is the eyes of the dead pharaohs, the eyes of the Moai on Easter Island, as dark as the soul but with a star of life inside,' Celia had said of the stone. The obsidian stone seemed to focus some sort of power, but I didn't know if I was strong enough to use it again, it took so much out of me. Or even if I *could* use it again.

The large black iron gates of the New York City Marble Cemetery had already been forced open, and I hightailed it inside to see that there were tall monuments marking the locations of underground graves – graves which were already being disturbed, from the inside out. I could hear the knocking on marble, feel the agitation beneath the soil. But where was the necromancer? I could not see him, yet green mist clung to the grass and the monuments, and I could hear the dead threatening to rise beneath my feet. They had already been called.

I steadied myself. 'As the Seventh, I command you.

Be still! Return to your slumber!' I shouted to the empty cemetery. 'I command you!'

The ring burned, my eyes stung from the pain. *Darn it!* I could feel the flesh swelling up under it.

'As the Seventh, I command you to return to your slumber!' I repeated, focusing with all my strength on my words, my intent.

Gradually the last remnants of glowing green mist vanished and the cemetery grew dark and silent. The earth beneath my feet became still. No knocking. No shrieking. No green fog. Everything had returned to normal, it seemed. Well, apart from the broken gates.

I closed my eyes and took a breath.

That was close ... Too close. It had been hard enough to turn back a few hundred of them. Imagine if thousands of the dead had risen up?

Above me came a distinctive rustling sound. The air shifted and when I opened my eyes a black shape descended, landing just inches in front of me.

Deus.

'Now, we must get to Spektor,' he told me in his deep, rich voice, grinning as always. He placed his hands on my slender shoulders and I found myself smiling back at him, eye to eye, drawn to those full dark brows and long, lovely eyelashes of his, and the light in his eyes that seemed to dance ...

'I commanded them to return to the ground,' I managed, closing my eyes and replaying in my mind what had happened. 'I actually did it! They crawled right back into the soil and the earth closed up around them. I've never seen anything like it!'

'Your great-aunt needs us, Pandora English,' Deus said. There was urgency in his voice.

I looked up and found myself caught in his intense gaze again.

'The necromancer is already at Central Park,' he told me. 'He will be in Spektor in no time. Get on my back. Now.'

The ancient Sanguine turned around and urged me onto him, and this time I didn't hesitate. I undid the buttons on my coat and climbed up, throwing my arms around his shoulders. I buried my face into the back of his neck, locking my hands around his hard chest and gripping his hips with my legs. We took off into the air in a breathtaking rush, my hair blowing straight back. In seconds we were far above the cemetery, the streets shrinking away.

'There are groups of people down there, walking and driving around like they're in a trance,' I told him after a minute, shouting against the whistling wind as we flew above the streets.

Deus turned his head so I could see the profile of his classical features and sensual mouth. I had to stop staring at him even as we rocketed over Manhattan. *Darn that blood he gave me*, I thought as I stared.

'I erased them,' he called back to me. 'They will be fine by now, acting perfectly normal, but they won't remember any of what they have seen.'

Of course.

I kept my chin nestled into his shoulder as we sailed over Manhattan, winging over towering skyscrapers and passing banks of windows so close I thought I might faint. In a heartbeat we flew past the observation platform of the Empire State Building, eighty-six floors above the street, moving as a dark shape, unseen by the tourists who looked out over the edge.

'Does anyone ever spot you?' I asked, as we banked again and flew down over the tall trees of Central Park.

'When I am flying? It is uncommon,' Deus said. 'Human perception rarely allows for such things.'

And those who might remember could be easily erased, it seemed.

'Would you ever ... erase me?' I dared to ask him.

I felt his chest shake under my hands and thought I heard a low chuckle beneath the din of the wind. 'I fear I could not do such a thing.'

'But you erased all those people down there.' *From the air. Like it was nothing.*

'And you would lump yourself in with them? You, who commanded the dead to return to their graves?'

Well, I guess I was a little different.

At the far northern end of the park I spotted the distinctive green glow again, and my stomach turned as cold as ice. A sense of terrible dread filled me even before we saw that the zombies were there below us, moving in lines through Central Park – a horde of skeletons walking on fleshless legs of yellowing bone, joined by Manhattan's recent dead, who groaned and shambled along, their wounds still oozing.

At a guess there were at least three hundred of them, maybe more, green mist swirling at their feet and disappearing into the tunnel that led to Spektor. There would be more on the other side.

This is bad. Very, very bad.

Barrett and the necromancer were nowhere to be seen, though I felt sure they were there, leading this grim march forward.

'We can be grateful you turned so many back,' Deus shouted. 'And that most of the cemeteries were moved off Manhattan Island. If we were in New Jersey ...' He shook his head. 'We'd have a much bigger problem on our hands.'

At that moment I could not imagine a bigger problem. 'Pandora ...'

'What—'

My words were pulled from me as our course changed suddenly. We plunged through the air, freefalling towards the ground, and I hung on, screaming, my arms and legs locked so tightly to Deus's body they hurt. We dropped fifty feet straight towards the treetops and then levelled out again only feet away from our deaths. Or mine, at least.

'The spell. I'm too close ...' Deus said as he flew erratically, moving up and sideways, trying to avoid the trees. The necromancer appeared just below us, from behind the foliage, holding both arms up in the air, fingers spread and palms pointing right at us.

He was controlling Deus.

'No!' I cried as we plunged again. We broke free again

and veered sideways, just missing the treetops. Deus was fighting the spell, but now the necromancer was far too close.

Deus could feel it, he'd said. But I could see it.

'To the left!' I shouted to him and he did as I said. We hit a narrow break in the green mist and Deus winged upwards.

'Stay left for another fifty feet or more! Now, up, straight up!'

We flew straight into the clouds above the park, freeing ourselves of the reach of those deadly green tendrils. Once we were safe we levelled off, and immediately headed for the thick fog surrounding Spektor.

CHAPTER
SIXTEEN

$\mathcal{M}$y home of Spektor was host to a most dreadful sight. The dead filed through the streets in lines, moaning and shuffling, stumbling in their rotten burial suits and gowns, all headed for Number One Addams Avenue, where hundreds of their kin already pressed at the iron gates and the mansion door, knocking and pounding with their bony fists. Some actually climbed the sides of the mansion, at times losing their footing and slipping down, their bodies coming apart like broken puzzles of bone on the pavement below before somehow reforming and starting again. Others pulled boards off the windows on the second floor and succeeded in crawling inside, their skeletal bodies fitting through small cracks.

I hung on to Deus, peering down as we flew overhead. *The dead want to get inside. They want to open the portal.*

He flew us to the peaked roof of the mansion and landed smoothly. I climbed off him somewhat reluctantly – even after our encounter with gravity in Central Park. The mansion didn't seem a good place to be right now.

'The protection spell won't work for much longer,' said Deus. 'Not once the necromancer arrives.'

It looked to me like it had already failed.

Below us the dead grew louder, and now their voices became clearer to me. Though their moans and cries were not like any human language, I came to understand their collective meaning. Many were chanting together, I now realised, using an ancient tongue. The necromancer seemed to be controlling them, as if they were one large organism chanting his words. They wanted to free their brothers and sisters in the Underworld below the house on which we stood. They wanted to set their brothers and sisters on the world of the living, every spirit, every corpse free to roam the streets of New York. The city would be overrun. The *earth* would be overrun, the balance of the dead and living destroyed. Without that balance there could be no life on earth.

I heard a crack, and the splintering of wood. The heavy mansion door would soon buckle.

'Hurry!' said Deus.

We ran across the roof tiles and he pulled open the door on the turret.

'I cannot come with you. I must stay clear of its reach. I have grown powerful over the centuries. If it can control me, use me against you ...'

'I understand. Thank you,' I said.

I ran inside the mansion, down the curving stairs, and when I reached the penthouse level I burst into the antechamber, leaping out of the casket. 'Celia! Celia?' I cried. Candles burned, the room smelled of incense, but she was not there. I ran to the lounge room. She was not in her usual spot in her reading chair, of course. She would be fighting off the necromancer downstairs. I pulled open my bedroom door and snatched Lieutenant Luke's sword from under my bed. I unwrapped it and admired the blade for a brief moment.

Here goes.

As I raced back across the penthouse I stopped and turned to look at the plethora of strange artefacts on Celia's shelves. There was something there – something my subconscious was drawn to. I stopped in my tracks, closed my eyes and concentrated for a moment. The two-headed coin flashed into my mind and I snatched it from its glass case and pocketed it, not sure what use it could possibly be. As I passed near the black widow spider in her little glass cage, I yelled, 'Don't look at me like that! I know what I'm doing!'

I ran with Luke's sword – well, it was more of an awkward jog, the thing was very heavy – out the front of the penthouse, and I looked down over the railing. Sure enough, my great-aunt was standing her ground in the lobby, her arms held out, chanting something I could not decipher, while that terrible green mist poured in through the thin gap under the door. It gathered around her at a distance of a few feet, in a perfect circle, held back by some invisible force. There was no mistaking the sound of the dead beating on the door with their fists and feet. I needed to get down there fast. The elevator was not an option, obviously. Posthaste, I made my way around the landing and was about to duck into that dodgy, unmaintained stairwell when I heard a loud crack. I looked back over the railing just in time to witness the heavy front door finally yield, toppling backwards and landing on the cracked tiles of the lobby.

Oh no.

'Celia, I'm coming!' I yelled, and bolted into the stairwell.

The stairwell was dark and though I'd forgotten to bring the torch there was simply no time to go back and look for it – not with Celia down there dealing with the invading dead. I held the sword in one hand and kept my other hand on the rail, holding on tight in the darkness as I negotiated missing stairs and stumbled over rotting planks and splintering wood. Finally I reached the fallen mezzanine door that Vlad had dutifully chopped down, and by the time I ran down the steps into the lobby, I could see that the situation was very bad indeed.

Hundreds of them were inside already.

'The necromancer is here,' my great-aunt Celia said, spotting me. 'We mustn't let it find the portal!'

The lobby of the mansion was overrun with the not-so-mortal remains of half of Manhattan but, still, there was that clear circle around Celia. The walking corpses – some without arms, one even without a head – filed around her as if she were a pillar, the mist circling but not able to close in. They began to pound on the hidden door beneath the mezzanine stairs.

Oh dear.

'Where is the portal?' I called out.

Celia shook her head, her arms still held out, palms

open. 'It is below the basement, but beyond that I don't know,' she told me. 'I have long suspected it was here but I have never seen it.'

I feared that would change tonight.

'They seem to know,' I said as the door under the mezzanine steps broke down under their fleshless fists. The creatures pushed the door aside and filed in tightly, one by one, doubtless headed for the basement and below. I felt sure the necromancer had discovered the position of the portal in his time here, and had waited until this night to use the strange magick of Friday the thirteenth to aid his powers and open the entry to the Underworld. But if Celia was right, the magick could go both ways.

There was still hope.

'I'll follow them!' I said. 'I'll stop them from getting the portal open.'

Somehow.

By now the green mist was no longer circling Celia, but moving past us into the dark corridor, pushing the dead onward on their mission. I really didn't want to go in there but I had no choice. I marched up to the small door, where the zombies passed close to me to squeeze themselves inside. I took a deep breath and held it, as if that would help, then shut my eyes and shoved myself between the corpses. In seconds I was being pushed along between the rotting bodies in that dank corridor, the strong stench of decay surrounding me. I was tightly sandwiched between a man in a tatty top hat and half a suit, and a woman holding a tied bouquet of dried stems, the flowers long since rotted away. In the low light I could see through the man's suit jacket through his ribcage and out the other side.

I took a breath and gagged.

'Pandora, I am here,' a familiar voice said. Celia had followed me inside. I tried to turn but I couldn't quite catch sight of her behind the wall of ... of ... *Ugh.* (Best not to look, I decided.) Nonetheless, I sensed that my great-aunt was only a few 'people' behind me, and I felt her intense dislike of our predicament like a little beacon indicating her proximity. It would have taken a lot for the ever-elegant Celia, of all people, to enter this disgusting, narrow passageway, considering the crowd that currently filled it.

'Zombies don't really eat brains, do they?' I asked her, hopeful. So far they seemed not to take any interest in our presence. I could only hope it remained that way.

'They are dead,' she replied. 'They don't need to eat, unless their master tells them to.'

Right. Well, let's hope the necromancer doesn't have that in mind.

By now the light coming through the open door from the lobby had faded from sight, and while the glowing mist that covered the floor of the corridor made it harder to negotiate the uneven stone, it did help to illuminate my way, acting as a lit pathway and casting spooky shadows up the walls and across the skeletal faces and bodies surrounding me. I sure hoped that mist had not already reached the portal, along with the necromancer.

'Darling, can you get ahead?' Celia asked from behind me.

'I'll try,' I shouted back.

I held up Luke's cavalry sword and tried to muscle in, which should not have been too hard considering the distinct lack of muscle – and flesh – in that twisting corridor. But it was a supernatural strength that animated these creatures, not physical strength. Moving forward seemed impossible. Celia was right though, we had to somehow get to the front of the pack and, if possible, block the rest from continuing on.

'Stop! I command you!' I yelled, but they did not so much as pause. The necromancer's power here was stronger than mine. 'I command you to stop!' I said again, and the corpses continued forward, set on their mission. I realised it would take more than my shouting to make them halt.

But what if I didn't have to actually make them *stop* at all?

'I command you to let us pass!' I called out, and with that the dead nearest to us pushed to the walls, still moving, and let Celia and I through. I held my breath as we passed perhaps twenty-five putrid corpses, each of whom stepped aside to allow us passage. Eventually we ended up at the base of the stone staircase I'd found with Luke. Here the space was a bit more open and I took a deep breath of slightly less pungent air, relieved. Here, though, there were more of the dead. It seemed they were now pouring into the house from all sides.

'The laboratory is near here,' I told Celia. Were they heading to it? Why?

We followed the path of corpses around the corner

and saw that the door to Dr Barrett's laboratory was open, the creatures filing through. We squeezed inside and Celia took in the steel table and frightening metal chair with its heavy leather straps. She frowned. She had not seen the lab before. Over the table the large light was on and the wheel next to me was spinning slowly, as if moved by the same magick that powered the dead. I had the feeling this activity was a side effect of the energy swirling through the room. Green mist clung to the floor and curled around the strange objects. The frog, floating in the formaldehyde jar, jerked.

Barrett's army – the necromancer's army – were filing straight through to his study and out the other side. This, I feared, was it. The icy sensation in my guts told me that the Underworld was very, very near.

'I think the portal may be open,' I said, horrified.

So Barrett had built his laboratory right on it?

'Quickly,' Celia urged, and we rushed forward without hesitation.

Sure enough, a door in the charred study was open on its hinge, the lock seemingly broken. Incredibly, when I'd been here with Lieutenant Luke, I hadn't even noticed the door. I'd been entirely blind to its presence, though Luke had experienced that strong aversion to the energy of the portal. He'd begged to leave, I recalled. Where was he now? I stepped through what I feared was the portal to the Underworld, my breath caught in my throat.

Oh boy.

THAT is the portal.

The small door in Barrett's study opened up into a

cavernous subterranean space. Below me were perhaps twenty-five broad, cascading stone steps leading to a magnificent, echoing chamber of natural rock. The steps vanished into a shallow pool of still, sulphury-smelling water that reflected the fierce, dancing green flames of a series of wrought-iron torches, hung from the rock on either side of the natural underground chamber. Stalactites hung from the ceiling, dripping with ooze and glittering with the water's reflection. Everything swam with that circling green mist. The dead continued to file past me down the stairs, gathering in the shallow water.

Directly opposite, perhaps thirty feet into the cave, was a flat rock wall of great height with an enormous circular portal carved into it, surrounded by what appeared to be runes. On either side of the portal were hundreds of skulls and femurs stacked up in a strange, twisting design, not unlike the double helix, and two frightening stone statues – one male and one female. Each was equally menacing, with the muscled bodies of Olympians and huge death's heads above their shoulders. They carried what looked to be ten-feet-high gold staffs.

I gaped.

This cave was, without question, the most beautiful and terrifying thing I had ever seen.

My great-aunt's cool hand touched mine, breaking me from my awe. 'We must stop it. Now.'

Indeed, he, or it, was there at the portal, hovering above the water at the giant door, chanting the words I'd sensed in all those gathered dead, the words I could not decipher into any known language, yet understood –

words that commanded the dead to open the portal and reunite the decaying bodies with their spirits. He wished to open the portal and have the dead overrun the living inhabitants of the Upperworld, claiming their domain.

The zombies gathered at his back, where Dr Barrett hung limply, clearly unconscious.

'I command you to stop!' I shouted to the necromancer with more confidence than I felt, holding Lieutenant Luke's sword in the air.

It turned around to face me – along with its gathering army – and those awful glowing eyes met mine. It spread its arms and my hair started to rise, electrified.

Oh, crap.

Celia and I ducked down, covering our heads as the creature clapped those withered hands together and shrieked, sending a blast of foul air through the chamber. The force of it rocked me backwards into Celia, and when it had passed I uncurled myself and stood up again. I wasn't going to stand for that. Sword in hand, I marched down the steps and into the water.

Oh, hell. Luke.

I saw my former friend amongst the gathering dead, his eyes lit green within that handsome, spectral face I'd once found so beautiful. He began to move towards me, his hands outstretched like claws. I had no doubt of his motives. He had been commanded to kill me once and for all.

'Lieutenant Luke, stand down!' I commanded, holding out his sword. I saw those eyes flicker blue for an instant, before he continued to march towards me.

Celia was at my back. 'Beware, Pandora,' she said. 'The necromancer is very powerful here. His magick is far stronger than mine.'

Behind Luke the necromancer was chanting again, and now he reached around in a most unnerving move of double-jointed dexterity, motioning for his followers to gather closer and hold up their arms (those who had arms, anyway). He began to shriek and I covered my ears.

Double-jointed . . . double-headed . . .

I pulled the two-headed coin from my pocket. 'I have an idea,' I said to Celia.

Did I?

'Yes,' she said, on seeing it. 'The coin. Good thinking.'

I examined the heads on both sides. The coin looked very old, though I could not see a date.

'Bring me a flame,' Celia said, seeming to read my own subconscious better than I could. I gave Luke's sword to her and dashed down the stairs and towards the nearest section of wall, wading knee-deep through the water. Stretching high, I reached up with both hands and pulled one of the heavy torches from the rough cave wall.

I looked over my shoulder. The runes were beginning to glow. Whatever the necromancer was doing, it was working. And Luke was still coming towards me.

'Quick. There is no time,' Celia shouted. 'Burn the coin on one side!'

I bit my lip. 'But which side?'

'Darling, I don't know! But it won't take much to find out. Quickly!'

I looked at the coin in my hand. The torch I was holding in my other hand was far too big, the flame too large and unpredictable. My hand would get badly burned if I held the coin over it. I looked around frantically for something to light with the torch – a smaller wick, a strip of cloth – but there was nothing in the cave I could use except my own clothing.

'What are you waiting for?' my great-aunt called out from the stone steps.

I closed my eyes and tried to focus on the coin. When I opened them again it was vibrating in my palm and lifting into the air. I felt veins pound in my forehead from the concentration, but if I could stop a whole elevator from crashing to the ground then I could certainly keep this small object in the air. I held the large flame beneath the coin, and back on the stairs my great-aunt chanted some strange incantation.

He is the coin, I told myself. *He is the coin.*

A wailing began, a terrible shrieking, and the necromancer turned and held its hands to its withered face. In seconds the green mist that had filled the cavern like a noxious vapour began to clear, the zombies slowing, their chanting – for the moment – stopped. The green flames of the torches turned crimson and orange. The spell was losing its power.

Lieutenant Luke had nearly reached me and now his arms fell to his sides and he blinked and shook his head. When he opened his eyes, I could see that they were blue again.

'Luke!'

I was so relieved that the singed coin dropped into my hand, and I screeched. It was almost too hot to hold. I ran to Luke, knowing there was no time to enjoy a reunion. 'Quick!' I said. 'While the necromancer is weakened, grab him!' I ordered, wielding the torch. 'Help us get him to the laboratory.'

With Luke's help, we dragged Barrett's limp body across the water and up the stairs into the laboratory. The necromancer's face was blackened and scorched, as if the torch's flame had burned him directly. We passed several corpses who stood around listlessly, seeming unclear of their direction. For now it seemed safe to ignore them, though I felt sure that would change if the necromancer revived.

'The chair,' I said. 'We can strap him in while we think of what to do.'

With considerable effort, we positioned Dr Barrett in the big metal chair, the sleeping doctor facing outwards. The thick leather straps would probably hold him, at least for a while. Celia buckled down one arm while I did the other, and Luke worked the straps on his footless legs.

The doctor woke just as I knelt down and helped Luke with the final strap. 'The passenger you brought back with you ...' I began. 'He tried to open the portal.'

'Him?' he said, seeming surprised. Seconds passed as the doctor blinked and struggled with consciousness. 'Did he succeed?'

'No,' Celia said, sounding rather unimpressed. Her arms were crossed.

I ran to the study door and locked it shut, and likewise the laboratory door, trying to stave off the threat of further dead company. 'If he wakes again, he may succeed,' I said.

'This is too important. Do whatever you must,' Barrett told us. 'But quickly. The passenger is coming back.'

That was what I feared. But what could we do? I'd tried to combat its spell. I'd used the double-headed coin. I was about out of tricks.

'Wait,' said Celia. '*You* must rid yourself of this thing. *You* must let it go,' she said, pointing at Barrett accusingly.

'But how?' he said.

'You are holding on to him,' she declared, much to my surprise. 'You wanted his power. You evoked his spirit, *didn't you?*'

Barrett closed his eyes. He nodded, ashamed.

'You brought him here. Now you must give up this black magick of yours. Give up the power of necromancy. It is not yours to have.'

Barrett's mouth fell open. 'But—'

'Do not play the fool with me,' she said angrily. 'You summoned it of your own free will. But this dark being is a curse to you. It will consume you completely if you don't let it go.'

Dr Barrett's eyebrows pinched together, his face turning crimson. He looked on the verge of tears. 'But I didn't mean to—' he began, and then his head fell forwards again.

Oh no. 'It's waking again! Look out!' I yelled.

Sure enough, the necromancer came awake with a

tormented, high-pitched shriek, its white hair standing up like a crown of vipers. The metal chair shook and rattled and I watched with peculiar horror as the passenger tried to look at us with its body strapped to the chair backwards, the legs and arms bent in the other direction – in Barrett's direction. Those hands and clawlike fingers flexed and the arms shook as it struggled against the thick leather binds.

The chair was bolted securely to the floor, but those straps were not going to hold.

The laboratory quickly filled with green mist again. I saw the tendrils of its spell sweep across the floor, circling the feet of the few listless zombies in the room, and under the lab door into the mansion corridor. It let out another shriek to summons the dead and turned its head at an unnatural angle to glare in the direction of the laboratory door.

Oh no.

I braced myself. 'Get back!' I cried. 'Look out for the door.'

There came a crashing sound beyond the closed door and something landed just on the other side. Something that filled me with intense cold. 'Look out, Celia!' I shouted. Lieutenant Luke seized me, eyes green, just as the door to the laboratory burst open, shattering in splinters.

Deus.

The ancient Kathakano stood in the doorway of the laboratory, framed by glowing mist, and looking more fierce and frightening than even I could have imagined.

His enormous ivory fangs – which I had never seen bared – were displayed in a terrible grin. The spell had caught him, just as he'd feared.

My great-aunt turned to the doorway and took in the sight of her Sanguine friend. '*Bugger*,' I heard her say under her breath. 'Dr Barrett, you've got until the count of three. One …'

She held up Luke's sword.

'Two …'

Deus flew in from the doorway towards her, fangs bared, and my great-aunt turned swiftly on her heel and cleaved the necromancer's head off with one confident swipe of Luke's sharp sword.

Holy hell in a handbasket. With kittens, I thought as the head on Barrett's back fell and flaked away to ashes even before it hit the ground. Deus already had Celia bent back in a dip, her black hair sweeping the floor and his lethal fangs inches from her throat.

'Three,' she said, in a slightly strained voice.

Luke let go of me instantly, the spell broken, and Deus, realising what he was about to do, righted my great-aunt immediately and took a step back, gaping.

'Madame, I am so sorry,' he said, and his fangs slid neatly back under his lips.

'I should hope so,' my great-aunt replied, and adjusted her widow's veil. 'Don't ever do that again.'

The green mist dispersed again as quickly as it had come. The zombies in the room fell to the ground with a clatter, now looking, well, properly dead. The necromancer at Barrett's back was dust. And Barrett? We looked down at him, waiting for some sign. The doctor's head hung lifelessly.

'I may have rushed him slightly,' my great-aunt admitted.

I bit my lip. She had warned him at least.

But after about a minute Barrett coughed and raised his head, and I exhaled with relief.

'Now may I suggest that you do not evoke dark beings again, doctor?' Celia said, before he even had the chance to speak.

He nodded weakly. 'Ma'am, I'll take that under advisement.' He straightened up a little, still strapped into the chair. 'It's gone now, isn't it? I can feel it.'

'Yes, it is. Let's see your eyes,' I said, and leaned in. Barrett's eyes were brown, with little yellow flecks in them. No glowing green. 'I think it's safe to unstrap him.'

Luke and I undid the straps and Barrett stood up unsteadily. He looked sheepish. My great-aunt was still frowning at him, her arms crossed. 'You could have started the revolution of the dead,' she told him. 'All on your own.'

He looked humbled. 'If it comes,' he said, 'it will not be my doing. But for what you have been through today, I truly apologise. I was foolish to come here with that being, though I swear I did not know what it would do.'

Celia narrowed her eyes. She seemed none too pleased with him.

'What were you doing when you died?' I asked, for lack of a better term for his condition. 'Was it just a fire?' I had to know.

'That was no ordinary fire, though I think you already know that,' he explained. 'I spent two decades trying to figure out how to open that portal, trying to learn the secrets of the dead. I got more than I bargained for.' He frowned, thinking of something that troubled him. 'I caused my wife much sorrow. It is a long time ago now, and I took my journals with me, so that no others could follow in my footsteps. I concede I made mistakes, but I have discovered worlds I'd only ever dreamed of. I made sacrifices, some of them great.' He looked to my great-aunt, who still had her arms crossed. 'You are the master of this house now. I know you wish me to leave. But if you permit me, I would like to return one day.'

Celia nodded, her mouth still turned down.

The master of the house. Funny how 'mistress' and 'master' meant such different things, I thought. I wished Barrett would stay and tell me more – more about the house, more about his travels – but Celia seemed eager to have him move on.

'Thank you, Pandora English, the Seventh,' he said.

'But where will you go?' I asked.

'There are many places.' Barrett smiled to himself, recalling things I could not even begin to imagine. 'My wife is calling me. I must say my goodbyes to her.'

'We'll leave you then, Dr Barrett,' I said. It seemed the right thing to do to give them their privacy. I walked out to the empty doorway – there were a lot of broken doors in the house now – and stepped into the corridor.

'Use that key wisely, Pandora English,' he said as we left him.

Oh dear. It had been in the satchel – the satchel I had lost in the cemetery. Where was it now?

We left Dr Barrett in his laboratory, and as I turned away I caught a glimpse of his wife at his side, dressed in her mourning clothes. The sight of them together touched something inside me with a deep sadness. Celia and I walked up the stairs with Luke and Deus towards the penthouse. I was exhausted and I knew it would be some time before I could process all that I had seen.

'I don't know about you, but I could use a good cup of tea,' my great-aunt said.

'Great-Aunt Celia, how did you know it would work? That cutting the head off the necromancer wouldn't destroy Dr Barrett?' I asked.

'I didn't,' she admitted quietly. 'Come on, let's go.'

We sat in the candlelit antechamber, an unusual four-some – ghost, ancient Sanguine, telepathic witch and the Seventh – three of us sipping Celia's calming tea, at her insistence. (Lieutenant Luke could not consume food or drink unless he was in human form.) *Is Celia's tea a kind of potion?* I wondered for the first time. A kind of calming witch's brew? If so, it seemed to be working. In some real way it felt as if the four of us were members of some secret society, charged with keeping Manhattan safe. And perhaps we were. Celia's tea ritual felt strangely civilised after all the bared fangs and head chopping.

'There are some repairs to be made to the mansion,'

she said matter-of-factly after the feeling in the room had settled.

That was an understatement.

'We can get to all that later, but for now there is another pressing issue to discuss while we have you and Deus in the room together. Deus?'

I cringed. I really wasn't up for any more pressing issues. What I needed was a good lie down – for about a month. I didn't think I'd be able to keep my eyes open for much longer, now that all that adrenaline had passed.

The grinning Kathakano turned to me and I recalled, with a shiver, the look of those fangs of his. 'Miss Pandora, I have been told that Harriet tried to kill you this evening? Is this true?'

I frowned. Let's see. The thing on Barrett's back tried to kill me. Luke tried to kill me. Deus tried to kill Celia. Was I forgetting anyone? 'Sorry, who?'

'The one you know as Redhead,' my great-aunt explained, and took another sip from her cup.

'Oh. Yes, she did.' It was hard to believe that was the same night. 'In the lift.'

Deus nodded gravely. 'I see. Then she has broken a direct order, and an important rule of this house. She must be dealt with accordingly.'

'Okay,' I said. For the moment the issue of my attempted assassination seemed about the furthest thing from my mind, though it was sort of an issue, wasn't it? Not quite on the level of the dead overrunning the planet but, yes, a problem.

Deus said nothing further about it, though I could tell

he was considering what to do. It seemed to me that his role in the Sanguine community was one of considerable authority. Judge and jury? Commander? We remained quiet for a while longer and my mind drifted back to the sight of that extraordinary subterranean cavern and that huge portal, which had – for now – remained closed. If only just.

Lieutenant Luke's ghostly hand came over to rest on mine and I flinched. He'd tried to kill me a few too many times lately. I knew it wasn't really his fault, but still, I was spooked. He pulled his hand away. I did not look at him.

Celia watched my body language and I sensed that she knew what was happening. She placed the empty cups on her silver tray. 'Now, come, Pandora,' she said. 'There is much to do. They need to be returned to their resting places before the sun rises.'

'What?'

'The dead,' she said simply. 'Deus, you have work to do also.'

'Indeed,' he agreed. 'Thank you for the tea. My apologies again for the incident in the laboratory.'

It *had* been awfully close.

Celia nodded. 'Apology accepted.'

'Now I will leave you, and begin my work in the city. Madame Celia, Miss Pandora, the Seventh.' He rose and bowed his head, and before I knew it he had opened the casket and stepped inside. In seconds he was gone.

Celia picked up the tray and led me to the door of the antechamber. I noticed Lieutenant Luke hesitate. 'You can help Vlad with the mansion repairs,' my great-aunt said, not quite looking in his direction. She could not see his face drop.

'Miss Pandora?' Luke said, still standing in the middle of the small room.

'Thank you, Lieutenant Luke. Thank you for your help tonight. I'll see you soon,' I told him, and bit my lip as he vanished instantly. Part of me was relived and the other part hated what this whole incident had done to us. My stomach twisted and I took a breath.

'Everything will be fine,' my great-aunt assured me.

We put the tray in the kitchen and the cups in the sink, and Celia led me to the tall lounge room windows overlooking Addams Avenue. To my dismay I saw that Manhattan's recently animated dead lay around the street outside the mansion on their backs and their sides, some heaped one upon the other, however they had fallen when the necromancer's spell was finally broken. It was a mess.

'You can do it, Pandora,' she said, with her hand on my shoulder.

'*I* can do it?'

'Command them to return to their resting places.'

'I won't ... anger them?'

'They have been pulled here. They cannot simply be left. It would not be right.'

I sighed. Well, I supposed my great-aunt was right about that.

It would be a long night.

CHAPTER
SEVENTEEN

*O*n Saturday morning the sun rose as usual, and beyond the thick fog surrounding Spektor, the (living) residents of Manhattan went about their business as if nothing had happened. I, for one, knew better, and after a night spent commanding the dead I did not feel like getting out of bed. I shut the heavy drapes on the four-poster bed, rolled over and passed out again.

I finally showered and dressed at noon, my eyelids still heavy despite the sleep in, and as I left my room I glanced back to see the edge of Luke's sword sticking out from under my bed. It gladdened me to see it there, protecting my bed, but it also made me think of the problems between Luke and I. It sure was nice to have him back to normal, blue eyes and all, but I was still a bit scared of him after all that had happened. And I would probably think twice before insisting that he leave the house for me. Sure, it might have been all Dr Barrett – or his passenger – but I'd pushed Luke into it and it hadn't ended well. If I really did have the powers of a necromancer, I didn't want to use my influence frivolously or for my own selfish reasons. (Was there a necromancer's ethics guide out there somewhere?)

A note from Celia in the kitchen gave me the good news that the city was suffering from collective amnesia. Deus had discovered my satchel in the cemetery and returned it. He was apparently confident that his mission to erase the living witnesses in Manhattan was successful – there would have been a few shocked folks in Central Park, I imagined – and Vlad had repaired the front door of the mansion and even the gates of the two marble cemeteries, leaving them in somewhat better condition than they had been in for a while. Would anyone notice the complimentary restoration, I wondered?

Celia's beautifully handwritten message ended with a postscript:

> *PS. I suggest you keep the skeleton key on you at all times. Perhaps this will help?*
> *Sincerely,*
> *Your Great-Aunt Celia*

Sitting atop the note was a thin, shimmering gold chain. I lifted it with one fingertip and marvelled at the way the afternoon light hit it. My battered satchel was sitting in the centre of the kitchen table, and I fished out the key, threaded it through the chain and slipped it around my neck. Yes, it was a good idea to keep the key close, now that we knew what it was.

I have the key to the Underworld around my neck.

We'd have to fix the door to the laboratory and Barrett's study, and make sure that one stayed firmly locked. And no one else must get the key. Perhaps Celia and I could even perform some sort of protection spell so that the door into that subterranean chamber couldn't be forced open again.

I grabbed my coat from the Edwardian hat stand and briefly examined my puffy eyes in the small oval mirror. Sure, I looked pretty underslept, but I didn't really look like I'd flown over Manhattan and spent the night battling the walking dead at the entry to the Underworld. I had a few scratches and a bit of a blister where the obsidian ring had burned me, but all things considered, I was okay. With the skeleton key around my neck and the torch in my hand, I stepped out of the penthouse, locked the door behind me and took the decrepit old stairs down to the mezzanine to survey the damage. Vlad (and Luke?) had sure been busy. The lobby had been swept out and the big front door was back in place, though I noticed the elevator was still not working. It would take a while for that to get fixed, I figured. Perhaps it was time to patch up the stairwell? I walked around the lobby, taking in the new scratches on the walls and cracks in the tiles.

Then I looked up and paused.

Finally Mrs Barrett had been released from the curse that had kept her here.

The chandelier was straight.

I slept in again on Sunday morning and through the evening I heard activity in the house – hammering, drilling. I examined the sword under my bed and wrestled with the idea of calling Lieutenant Luke, now that he was back to normal, but in the end I chose to spend the night alone, contemplating all I had learned.

Celia had informed me that Deus was trying to track down the four troublesome Sanguine, so that Redhead could receive whatever punishment he thought was appropriate, though frankly I suspected Athanasia had been involved as well. For now, though, it seemed that they were laying low and had not returned to Spektor.

I did not miss them one bit.

On Monday I used the computer at *Pandora* magazine to check the online news sites a few times throughout the morning, while sorting Pepper's emails, looking over my shoulder to see that I was not observed ('Walking dead + Manhattan' was an odd search term at a fashion magazine). Nothing related came up, which seemed incredible to me. I'd already noticed that over the weekend the local newspapers seemed to have reported nothing of the strange events on Second Avenue, nor the memorable march of corpses through Central Park. Though Celia had told me that would be the case, it still amazed me. Evidently Deus had done his job well. It was not the first time his considerable skills had been employed to keep supernatural secrets, of course.

The whole thing made me wonder just how much went on that we did not hear about.

One person in Manhattan who had not been erased, however, was Jay Rockwell. (Well, not again, anyway.)

Jay walked into the *Pandora* office at 11:59 a.m. on Monday, and Morticia, who'd already pulled out her bagel for lunch, sat up suddenly and exchanged a few words with him at reception, giving me a minute to absorb his surprise arrival and think of what to say. I hadn't even sent him a text yet, I realised. *Oops.* The phone reception in Spektor was nonexistent but that was still no excuse. I could have made the effort to find a patch of reception in Central Park to send a hello at the very least.

He walked to my cubicle, smiling (which did bode well, I thought), while behind him Morticia made big eyes. The proverbial cat was out of the bag, it seemed. There would be questions later, I knew.

'I'm so sorry about Friday night,' I said, standing up to greet him. Jay towered over me in my flat shoes and I had to admit that I liked the surprise visit. 'I hope you will forgive me for running off.'

He took my hand in his and it felt so warm that I realised I'd grown more accustomed to the feel of the undead, or Lieutenant Luke's ghostly embrace, than the feel of a real, living, warm-blooded man. 'I've been worried about you,' he told me. 'It sounded like something serious was going on.'

He searched my eyes for something, though I wasn't sure what.

'Yes, it was quite urgent. My great-aunt …' I began, but trailed off. I thought of Celia holding back the dead. And then chopping the head off Barrett's pesky passenger-parasite. And then being attacked by Deus, his fangs bared. I decided not to try to explain further, and I just smiled, my chin tilted up to Jay's face. 'But everything is fine now. Again, I'm really sorry,' I said.

'I'm sure you'll make it up to me somehow,' Jay told me, with a cheeky smile. 'Are you going somewhere for lunch?'

'Well, I wasn't planning to.' I'd packed a sandwich.

'I'd like to chat with you about something, if that's okay,' he said, and I thought I detected something a bit vulnerable in his voice.

Hmmm.

'Okay. Sure,' I said. It was already noon, so I put my coat on and grabbed my satchel, both of which looked a bit grubby after my recent adventures, I noticed. There were faint grass stains and dirt on the sleeves of the camel-coloured coat (Ingrid Bergman's dress needed a bit of love, too, that's for sure) and some part of me panicked a bit, imagining that Jay would think I'd spent some hours rolling around in the grass since our date. 'Perhaps we can sit in a park,' I suggested, and crossed my arms to cover the stains.

We left the *Pandora* office, Morticia staring at us as we went, and Jay Rockwell ordered a hotdog from a vendor on the street outside, which I can't imagine was a common meal choice for someone like him. We carried our lunches a few blocks and found an empty bench in Duarte Park in a patch of spring sunshine. The trees around us were coming to life after a cold winter, and the change of weather brought out the warblers and other birds. It was lovely.

'Pandora, I wanted to tell you that I think you're really different,' Jay said as we tucked into our lunches.

I stiffened a little. 'Oh?'

He turned towards me on the bench, his hotdog in his lap. 'It's probably no secret that I have dated a lot of women. You can judge me for that, but I want you to know I've never met anyone like you.'

It had not escaped my attention that he was rather popular with women. I didn't know how to respond.

'Somehow I feel like I've known you before,' he continued.

I licked my lips. There it was again. The deja vu stuff. Perhaps Elizabeth Bathory's henchwomen hadn't done such a good job of erasing his memory? Or maybe that always happened when you were erased – the memory went, but the emotion stayed? That seemed problematic, to say the least.

'Are you seeing a lot of women at the moment?' I asked, trying to make the question sound light. Like the 'friend' who was at the Empire State Building, I thought. I had asked him a similar question before, though that was a couple of months ago now, B.E. – *Before Erasure*. If we were to keep seeing each other I'd have to remember what was B.E. and what was P.E. – *Post Erasure*, so to speak.

Jay hesitated. 'I have been seeing a couple of women, but nothing serious. And not since our date, obviously,' he said, and then he laughed at himself, amused by the idea that he might have gone on another date since.

'I do hope you'll forgive me for having to fly off like

that,' I said. Of course I couldn't tell him just how literally I'd had to fly.

Jay leaned in, surprising me by becoming serious. 'Pandora, are you seeing the man who came to get you? Is he a boyfriend of yours?' he asked, and searched my face again.

Was I seeing Deus? So that's what this was all about.

'Oh, no,' I replied quickly. 'Not him. No, he is a friend of my great-aunt. I'm not with him at all.'

He relaxed a touch. Was that what he'd wanted to ask me? It seemed to be. I suppose Deus did leave quite an impression.

'He's a friend of your great-aunt? He looks pretty young.'

'You haven't met my great-aunt. She's ... um ...' *How could I put it?* 'Full of life.'

I didn't have a lot of time on my lunch break, so I tucked into my sandwich again, watching the cars and pedestrians pass. A woman with a poodle made her way past and the dog lifted its leg to urinate on a post. I looked the other way.

'You know you made me quite jealous, Pandora,' Jay said, and I paused with the sandwich at my lips.

I put my lunch down. 'I didn't mean to make you jealous but, now you mention it, I do have something important I need to say.' I shuffled around to face him, my knees touching his. This was as good a time as any, I supposed.

What was the best way to say this? To get the issue off my chest?

'Jay, I just need you to know that there *is* someone else in my life. I need to be honest with you about that. I was going to tell you, but I had to run off and I didn't get the chance.'

He frowned and appeared to brace himself for my news. 'Not the man who came to the restaurant?' he ventured.

'No. This other man in my life died some years back,' I said.

Not that Deus hadn't also died. Technically.

Jay's shoulders relaxed with that news. 'Oh. I'm so sorry to hear that.'

'But he is very special to me, regardless of his death,' I continued. 'I need to be clear. I hope that doesn't sound too strange?' I'd been thinking about the issue a lot over the weekend.

'I understand,' he said, though I doubted that was true, strictly speaking. 'It's not strange at all. Not a day goes by that I don't think about my mother.'

His mother had died of breast cancer. It was very sad. I took his hand in mine. 'Cancer is a terrible thing,' I said sincerely. 'That must have been so hard.'

Jay cocked his head. 'I didn't realise I'd told you about that.'

Oops.

He'd told me about his mother the first time we were at the Italian restaurant, not the second time. It had been B.E. *Darn it.* 'I understand what that's like,' I said, covering. 'Being an orphan, myself, I know it's hard to lose a parent, or both.'

Jay nodded.

'I just needed to let you know that I still care for this other ... man.'

'Of course.' He managed a smile. 'I hope you will tell me about him one day.'

'Maybe.' I looked at my watch. It was time to go. 'Look, I'm sorry to always be running off like this, but I should get back to work.'

We walked back to the *Pandora* office and Jay stopped me at the door outside. 'How about we do something on the weekend?' he said. 'Saturday night? Or are you busy?'

The idea did have appeal. 'Can I get back to you?'

Jay smiled and pulled me in close. I came up to his shoulder. 'Sure,' he said, and he tilted his head down and pressed his warm lips to mine. They tasted like candy, and I lingered there for a moment, enjoying the feel of his beautiful human kiss.

'I'll call you soon,' I said, pulling away and sprinting up the stairs with butterflies in my stomach.

I successfully dodged questions about Jay Rockwell's visit and tried to get as much done as possible in the afternoon. There were a lot of messages coming in for my boss about the upcoming fashion spread, and now that she'd chosen her models I put forward suggested looks for the first time, collating images from the Paris spring shows, which was a bit exciting. But at five thirty when Morticia and I left work together to walk to the subway, I knew there would be no escaping the questions. In my three months at the magazine I'd only twice admitted to going on any kind of date, so Jay's appearance at the office, twice now, was sure to come up.

'Are you seeing Jay Rockwell?!' she exclaimed excitedly when we were no more than a foot outside the office. It was as if she'd been holding on to those five words all afternoon.

There seemed no point in denying it. 'Yes, I am seeing Jay, but please don't tell anyone. It's not serious or anything. It was just a date.' Or two.

There was no point confiding that Jay was in fact 'roses guy', the unnamed man I'd dated before, and who'd sent a large bouquet to the office. That was B.E.

'What was it like?' she pressed, as we made our way down the stairs. 'Did it go well?'

I realised she might be mixing up my mysterious date to the Empire State Building the previous Thursday with the one I'd had on Friday, which I hadn't mentioned, but I went on anyway. 'It was nice, but I had to leave because of an emergency ... with my great-aunt,' I specified, when I saw her eyes widen. 'It's all fine now, but I guess he was worried and wanted to see if I was okay.'

'Are you?'

'Totally.'

We reached street level and she pushed open the door. The sounds of SoHo traffic hit us and we stepped onto the footpath. 'Will you see him again?' she asked, and shut the door behind us.

'I think so. He is really nice. But it's complicated.' I shrugged and gave a neutral smile, unsure how to explain.

I sure didn't like lying or being evasive. But I was doing it an awful lot. 'Hey, would you like to see a movie on Friday?' I asked.

'Sure. The new Burton? It sounds cool.'

'It's a deal.'

We walked into the crowd, headed for the subway. 'I like your necklace, by the way,' Morticia said. 'I haven't seen it before.'

'Thanks.' I pulled the chain up, so that the key showed above the neckline of my blouse. It felt strange to possess such a thing. *The key to the entrance of the Underworld.* 'It's from my great-aunt,' I said, and then I froze, stopping abruptly in my tracks. 'Um, I'll have to leave you here,' I told my friend.

Morticia went on, still talking, then realised she'd lost me. She spun around and came back to where I was standing. My gaze was fixed on a figure in the crowd – a figure I doubted she could see. 'What is it?' she asked, studying my expression.

'Nothing. Just … I forgot I'm meeting someone,' I said clumsily.

I could not believe what I was seeing. I almost could not speak.

'Are you sure you're okay?'

'Totally.' I'd felt the blood drain from my face, and now my cheeks grew as hot as if I were in front of an open fire. My heartbeat was behaving with equally erratic abandon. 'Go on,' I managed in a reasonably sane voice. 'I'm fine. Friday night is a date, and I'll see you in the morning.'

Morticia left me reluctantly to wander off into the rush hour crowd of pedestrians. When she was out of view I walked up to the familiar figure who was leaning against the brick wall of one of the buildings not far from the office, clearly waiting for me.

'Lieutenant Luke. How are you here?'

Luke was on the street, in SoHo, without the full moon, and without my help. He had that peculiar opaque quality about him, the appearance of being something real and yet not real, as if you might blink and find him gone, a mere trick of the light. In the soft light of the fading sun, he was even fainter than usual. The pedestrians around him clearly could not see that he was there, resplendent in his Civil War uniform, his cap held respectfully in his spectral hands. Only I could see him. I could see him perfectly.

'Miss Pandora, I am free,' he declared.

'Free?' I felt tears spring to my eyes.

'You and Celia have freed me from Barrett's spell. I can leave the house and I don't need to be flesh to do it.'

Despite the public setting I threw my arms around Luke's ghostly form, feeling the cool comfort that was not quite human. 'I'm so happy for you,' I whispered as he circled his arms around my waist. 'You deserve to be free.' I looked up and met his bright blue eyes – the eyes I'd so missed, eyes that no longer frightened me, I realised. 'Will you ... leave now?' I dared to ask. My throat had closed up and the words came out strangled.

If Luke was free and never returned to Spektor and the mansion that had been his prison, I should be happy for him. He'd suffered more than enough, and he deserved to be at peace. Any other response was just selfish. But still ...

Lieutenant Luke reached up and ran a ghostly hand over my hair, his blue eyes as intense and sincere as ever. 'I am your spirit guide, Pandora English,' he said. 'I am yours. I will never leave you, as long as you want me.'

I closed my eyes, awash with relief, and we held each other, the crowd passing us, indifferent. I must have looked like a crazy woman, weeping alone, but I may as well have been as invisible as Luke.

Goodness, my life is complicated, I thought, and wiped a tear from my cheek.

I straightened and pulled the satchel over my shoulder. 'Lieutenant Luke, you aren't going to go all green-eyed on me again, are you?'

He looked at me questioningly, and I wondered for a moment if he realised all he had done while he was under the spell of Barrett's necromancer. It seemed he did not.

'Well, then. Shall we walk?' I suggested, and took his hand. 'You're going to love this town ...'